The Crane Wife

A psychological thriller

Max China

Contents

Copyright

Cover by Akiragraphicz

Dedication

In memory of my parents, Elsie and Stefan, and my younger brother, Richard, who passed away in 2019.

In time, we'll meet again.

Acknowledgements

Special thanks to Elizabeth Lee, the talented author of the novel Cunning Women, for her helpful critiques as the book unfolded.

Thanks to Colin Meloy and The Decemberists for their musical and lyrical interpretation of the old Japanese fable, The Crane Wife. Listening to that song one rainy Sunday afternoon provided me with the inspiration to write this novel.

I'd like to thank everyone involved in creating this book. It's been a long time coming…

Chapter 1

Northwest Scotland Spring 2018

The hike was brutal, much harder than Jack expected. Three miles blitzed by icy winds and blinded by granulated snow, culminating in a thigh-sapping scramble up a steep rocky hillside.

On reaching the ridge, he knelt to catch his breath. After a minute, he rose to his feet and squinted ahead. The ravine he sought appeared in the fading daylight, dark and foreboding as it snaked across the landscape.

'Thank God,' he whispered.

The caves couldn't be far away. For a moment, he pictured his father sheltering inside them, huddled over a fire, waiting out the storm. 'Man alive, Dad,' he said under his breath. 'This place is *cold.*'

He picked his way closer to the gorge, careful not to trip, straining ahead, looking for the landmark outcrop that concealed an entrance into a cave system.

A gust of wind slammed him from behind. Propelled towards the drop as if shoved by a giant hand, he threw himself down, hands and feet scrambling for purchase. This is it, he thought. Inches from the edge, his heel jarred against a rock. Another inch, and he'd have fallen into the abyss.

Heart hammering in his chest, Jack stared at the leaden sky and, taking a moment to gather his wits, rolled onto his knees and crawled away from the ledge. Once he was safe, he pulled out his GPS. His eyes blurred; he rubbed them and peered at the screen. A blinking green location marker almost overlapped the purple destination dot. Nearly there.

The wind whipped through his flapping jacket, chilling him to the bone. He braced himself and stood. Where's the crag? Oh, Christ. It's on the other side. His spirits sank as he weighed his choices. Backtracking was not an option.

Startled by a sudden movement, he stifled a gasp as a magnificent red stag trotted into view. Unaware of his presence, it smelled the air raking the ground with a forehoof. Impulsively, he lifted his iPhone to take a picture. The beast raised his head. Through fogged breath, he and the stag stared at each other. Then, with a snort, it wheeled around and bolted. A split second later, a gunshot cracked.

Twenty yards away, a mound of snow-covered heather rose and shook like a dog coming out of a river. A green line scythed through the blizzard towards Jack. He lowered his gaze to his chest. A luminescent dot flickered over his heart.

A figure materialised out of the storm, as pixelated as a detuned image on an old analogue TV. Too big for a woman. Dressed in military-style camouflage, he wore a white ski mask with red stitching around the openings for his mouth and eyes. His rifle emitted a green laser beam.

The stranger stalked toward him, one of those tough-as-nails all-weather types. And a poacher, too. It was March, and the hunting season only lasted from July until October. Jack had a feeling he'd best not mention it.

'Hey there!' Jack yelled over the wind. 'Sorry about that. I didn't realise anyone else was up here.'

The man closed in, soldier-like, weapon up.

A spurt of adrenaline surged through Jack's veins. 'Can you put the gun down, please? You're making me nervous.'

The poacher continued his slow advance.

Jack blinked snow from his eyelids, breathed deep and lifted both hands. 'Look, I already apologised—'

'What the hell are you doing up here?' Anger infused the beady eyes.

'I'm looking for my father.'

High and shrill, the man mocked him. *'Looking for my father.'*

Fear thickened Jack's tongue, the taste metallic. He thought frantically, seeking to defuse the man's anger. 'You're American?'

'Shut your fucking trap!' The black muzzle jabbed forward, stopping inches from Jack's face.

'Told me I'm making a big kill today, and that's what I aim to do.' His finger tightened on the trigger.

Chapter 2

Five months earlier.

Jericho Mathers leaned precariously from the top of a twenty-foot ladder. One hand clamped around a rung while hammering timber sidings into place with the other. He couldn't work with anyone else banging around without cowering. A throwback to his soldier days. Handling lengthy boards and fixing them single-handedly was a technique his dad taught him. He smiled. The old man would have loved working out here with me in this Indian summer. It occurred that he'd known little of him. A soldier, he sacrificed his family life for foreign wars. Jericho's mother vowed she'd not allow her son to join the army, but when the time came, faced with his determination, she gave her blessing.

Late afternoon sunlight beamed a bright swathe between the house and surrounding trees, crossed the lawn, stretching beyond and into the newly ploughed fields. He looked down. His elongated shadow projected along a seemingly endless corridor, reaching for infinity.

Africa. A memory flared, quelled instantly, and left him teetering on the edge of the void of forbidden recollections. He switched to thinking about Anita. *Neet*. Imagined her in the distance, wrapped in white bedsheets as she was the morning she died. In his dreams, she often beckoned him.

Over the years, he'd considered joining her, but unconvinced of the existence of the hereafter, he put the idea aside. At least this way, she remained alive in his thoughts. Jericho sighed, descended a rung, and rolled out the crick in his neck. When did I get so old?

He squinted at the black weatherboarding, buttered soft and yellow by the setting sun, and moved the ladder, adjusting its rake against the wall. With one more siding left to fit, he climbed the rungs to measure the last section.

At the top, a commotion carried on a light breeze. Jericho glanced over his shoulder at the stand of trees behind.

Quarrelsome crows squabbled. Bad-tempered, they fought for the highest roost in the bone-white limbs of a dead tree; amid flying feathers, their furious caws rose to a crescendo.

Then silence.

The waning sun crowned the victor's head with gold. The bird seemed to glare at him, its eyes gilded and triumphant.

Something wet and cold dropped onto the back of his hand.

Snow. At this time of year?

Watch for the skelf...

A dream broke from his subconscious.

He froze at its unravelling.

Anita played swing ball in the garden with their two children while he tilled the vegetable patch. Their joyous laughter filled him with warmth.

'Come on, Jerry,' she yelled. 'You can finish that tomorrow. Jack's bored with beating Emily and me, so now he wants to play you. You'd better hurry before it gets too dark.'

He grinned, threw a handful of roots into a wheelbarrow, and scrubbed his hands on his overalls. 'Seven years old, and he thinks he can beat me?'

The little boy's face beamed as he puffed out his chest.

Shadows gathered on the periphery of Jericho's vision as he started towards his son. Thunder clouds descended, and the air felt heavy. Although Anita was forty yards away, he registered her consternation. He followed her gaze and turned to look behind. A dishevelled stranger, clothed in traditional highland garb, strode purposefully his way, long grey hair flying in the sudden breeze.

Mesmerised by the pendulous action of the stranger's sporran, Jericho thought he recognised the faded green and black tartan. 'Can I help you?' he said.

'It's getting late.' The man pointed westwards to the darkening sky. 'See, when the sun dips low and the first snow of the year falls on All Souls Day, ye cannot be outside.' He lapsed into Gaelic.

'Speak English,' Jericho said. 'Who are you?'

The highlander tossed his hair and ran a grubby hand through his long grey beard. 'Fillan's the name.'

Jericho's eyes narrowed. 'What do you want?'

Fillan scratched his cheek. 'To warn ye. He will come when snaw falls on the Day of the Dead.'

'Who will?'

'A wolf more terrible than ye can imagine.'

Jericho gauged Fillan's weathered features for clues to the man's sanity.

'Oh, I know what ye're thinking, laddie. There are no wolves in Scotland.'

He raised an eyebrow. 'You aren't making sense.' Anita was approaching, arms around Emily and Jack, their voices asking anxious questions. 'No more wolf talk,' Jericho said. 'Can't you see I've got young kids?'

The highlander nodded. 'That's why I came. Take yer woman and bairns far away from here. This creature is no snaw ghast. He is a *worricow*, a demon. When dusk falls, get inside. Lock all doors and windows. If ye don't, he will consider it an invitation and take ye up on it.'

Anita drew closer, mumbling reassurance to the children. 'It's okay. The man just got lost, and he's asking Daddy the way. Keep behind me.'

Fillan glanced at her, lowered his eyes, and tapped a finger against his nose. 'Watch for the *skelf*.'

'You mean the *snow?*' Jericho yelled after him as Fillan marched from his property onto the path skirting woodland a hundred yards distant.

Anita nodded in the highlander's direction. 'Who was that?'

'I'm not sure, but I can't shake the feeling I've seen him before.'

'I think you'd remember someone like that if you had,' she said. 'What did he want?'

'It doesn't matter. The guy's eccentric.'

15

'Maybe, but he scared my babies.' She laid a hand on his shoulder. 'Are you okay?'

Jericho forced a smile. 'Of course.'

On the surrounding trees, the last dry leaves of autumn rattled like tiny castanets. Turbulence parted the clouds, revealing a sliver of the moon. Anita shivered. A flurry of snow whipped through the air, driven by an icy breeze and, with it, a mournful howl. She seized Jericho's arm. 'What on earth was that?'

Together, they scanned the dusky treeline. Out of the shadows, something dark emerged.

'Grab the kids, Neet,' he said from the corner of his mouth.

She snatched their hands.

Eyes wide, Emily craned her neck. 'Is that a wolf?'

'I'm scared,' Jack said.

'That Scot just now,' Jericho whispered. 'He predicted this.'

Anita shook her head. 'That's ridiculous.'

Frightened and confused, the children sobbed.

'Hey, stop worrying. There aren't any wolves outside captivity. Besides, isn't that where our visitor entered the woods a few minutes ago?'

Jericho frowned. 'What do you mean?'

'Look at its size against the old tractor. It's as tall as I am.' She laughed without conviction, mostly to reassure the children. 'Whoever that is, he's just dressed up to scare us.'

16

The wolf shook a layer of snow from its long black fur, lowered its head, and stalked towards them with an air of nonchalance.

'No human dresses up and walks like that, love,' Jericho said, gauging the distance between the house, them, and the wolf. Tight. Could he buy them time? If he ran for the fork from the vegetable patch and it came after him, he'd kill it. What if it didn't chase him? Neet and the kids wouldn't stand a chance. 'Okay,' he said. 'No sudden moves. If we keep calm, we'll be indoors before it gets anywhere near.'

As one, they changed direction and made their way up the shingle path. Jericho walked backwards, watching the beast. Oh, Christ. To reach the front door, they had to pass a cluster of barns. For thirty seconds, he'd lose visual contact with the creature.

'Neet, run for it as soon as we're out of sight.'

'It'll hear us on the gravel,' she whispered.

'Yes, but you don't think it won't take advantage and close in while we can't see it?'

The outbuildings loomed before them. His wife and children entered the alleyway between the timber structures. They needed a head start. 'I'm watching you,' Jericho whispered, lingering at the corner, keeping the wolf in sight. The beast raised its head and cocked an ear as if it had heard him.

'Go,' he said, shooing them off.

'What about you?' she said.

'I'll be right behind you. Now, stop looking at me and *run!*'

A child in each hand, she took off, the kids tripping along

17

behind. 'Faster. Hurry,' she cried. The sound of their feet pounding the gravel seemed extraordinarily loud.

When he looked back, the wolf had gone. Oh shit. Jericho sprinted, mentally mapping the alley's intersection with the driveway leading to the front door. If his calculations were correct, when they glanced right, the wolf would be thirty yards away. Scooping Jack into his arms, he dashed alongside, his breath laboured. Five paces to go. Like running on a beach. Why did he put the shingle down so thickly? 'Whatever you do, when we hit the drive, don't look and do not stop. Head straight to the door.'

They cleared the cover afforded by the outbuildings, Anita and Emily on his left. Jericho glanced right, horrified.

The hurtling wolf had reduced the distance between them to just ten yards.

He put Jack down and shoved him. 'Quick, Neet, grab him. Get indoors.' He looked frantically for anything to use as a weapon. Nothing.

The beast closed in, panting clouds of vapour.

Anita raced to the door, opened it, and dragged the children inside. 'Get in, get in.'

Emily screamed, 'Dad! Come on!'

'Jerry, what are you doing?' Anita yelled. 'It's too big. You can't fight that.'

Arms and legs pumping, he sprinted, pitched himself through the door, and slammed it shut.

A moment later, the house thundered as the wolf slammed against it.

Fingers frantic, Jericho secured the lock. He propped his

back against the door while he caught his breath.

Wide-eyed, struck dumb by fear, Jack shivered. Urine pooled beneath his shoes. 'Is that the b-big bad wolf, Mummy?'

'We're safe now, little brother,' Emily said and wrapped her arms around him.

'Hey, hey.' Anita pulled the children close. 'It's all right. Daddy's calling the police. They'll come and catch it.' She shivered and said to herself, 'How is this even possible?'

'Oh no, Neet! The French doors. They're still open! Get the kids upstairs now!'

They sped up the stairs while Jericho dashed the length of the hallway, skidding on the quarry-tiled floor as he flew around the corner and through the opening into the back room. He slid to a halt.

The monster slunk in, head lowered, death gleaming from cold eyes. It paused and sniffed arrogantly. Hind legs tensed, the beast growled, baring yellow fangs then sprang at him.

Jericho sidestepped and slipped. A hand down to break his fall, he pitched sideways, rolled clear, scrambling on all fours, then to his feet. Jericho shot through the doorway into the hall, aware of the snap of the wolf's jaws at his heels. Once. Twice. Three times.

The animal snarled as it gave chase. Claws raking the floor, it closed in on him.

Jericho kept tight to the wall, sprinting back the way he'd come.

Paws scrabbling, his pursuer went wide.

If I can reach the front door, I'll lure it outside! He

thought and bolted through the hallway.

On the straight, teeth gnashing, the wolf gained ground.

It's too fast. I won't make it. Try the stairs! His right hand gripped the newel post, and he used it to pivot the corner in a tight arc.

Unable to take the turn at speed, the wolf overshot the stairway.

Silence followed.

Charging upstairs, Jericho glanced behind.

The wolf crouched at the bottom and leapt.

On the landing, sharp claws tore into Jericho's back, slamming him down.

The reek of blood and decaying flesh on the wolf's breath blew hot on his neck.

Tensed, expecting the fatal bite, he prayed Neet had called the police and that they'd arrive in time to save her and the kids.

Death beckoned him. Play possum! No other choice. His muscles forced to relax, he flopped. Offering his throat, he changed his mind. This thing won't respect surrender. His right elbow crooked; he stabbed the point of it into the creature's belly and twisted away onto his back. Teeth snapped at his face. Heart racing, Jericho drove his hands up, grabbing the thick mane beneath the animal's jaws. Frenziedly, it shook its head.

Bucking at the hips, he fought to free his legs. 'I can't hold him, Neet,' he cried.

Darker than night, its pinpoint pupils loomed ever closer, lasering evil intent.

Jericho's arms trembled with effort, his strength failing.

The creature opened its mouth.

He closed his eyes.

'Get off my husband!' Anita yelled, repeatedly smashing down a table lamp's brass stem on the wolf's skull.

Suddenly, the weight pinning him lifted. Too late, Jericho realised the wolf had gone for her. Snatching at its tail, he missed.

Anita clubbed the wolf again. The strike had no effect. She tripped as she backed up. It bit into her windpipe and ripped her throat out with a quick left and right shake.

Her screams echoed across the corridors of time. Just as her screams had summoned him into consciousness the morning she died, the nightmare had returned to ground him in the present.

Tears streamed down his cheeks. 'You saved me, Neet,' he whispered.

His head swam as he emerged from the fog of suppressed memory, gripping the ladder stiles with unnecessary force.

The sun dipped into the horizon, a light-bending trick, for, in reality, it had already gone.

Why remember all of this now? He glanced at the date in the bubbled window of his wristwatch. 2 November. The anniversary of the day she'd died. *The Day of the Dead.*

The highlander's warning echoed in his mind.

Watch for the skelf…

Jericho descended the ladder as fast as if he'd fallen.

Chapter 3

Jericho checked he'd locked the doors and windows with more care than usual. The air whistling through the window frames chilled him. He pressed his nose against the glass, squinting into the depths of the whirling snow, half expecting the wolf to emerge from the storm's myriad shape-shifting forms. Low moans blew down the chimney, deep and unearthly as if the old god Pan squatted there playing his pipes, the fluted notes varying with the intensity of the wind. Was that a distant howl? He listened intently.

Concluding it was nothing, he crossed the room to the fireplace. Lit a match, bent, and held the flame to the kindling, dropping it only when it burned the tips of his fingers. The wood caught, flared and licked the undersides of the logs; he sighed and watched the flames grow. A hint of smoke reached his nostrils, a familiar smell of wintergreen and leather. Satisfied it wouldn't go out, he placed a fireguard on the hearth. Residual moisture sizzled and spat, ejecting sparks from the crackling wood. He straightened, passed his hand over the horse brasses pinned to the mantle and glimpsed his reflection in the mirror. He grimaced. After a year without trimming his hair or beard, he bore a marked resemblance to the highlander from his nightmare. Jericho ran his fingers through the tangled salt and pepper thicket covering his chin, poured a whisky, and, raising it as if to an invisible audience, made a multidirectional toast. 'Absent friends,' he muttered before downing it in a single gulp. He made his way upstairs to change.

At the beginning of an alcoholic haze, he eased into a hot bath he couldn't recall running and turned off the taps. Engulfed in steam, he laid back and drifted.

Lulled by the warmth, consciousness abandoned him. His knees came up. He sank further into the water. Anita walked the bright galleries of his mind, her beauty ageless, forever preserved in her prime. The image slipped away. Darkness invaded his delusions. Warm liquid entered his mouth. He coughed himself awake.

Jericho sat up. Emptiness engulfed him. His tongue thick with whisky, he whispered, 'Anita, I remembered.'

Cold leached into his skin like the chill he'd felt when they'd lowered Anita's coffin into the earth. Oh boy. He wriggled up into a sitting position and placed his head between his knees.

The telephone rang, jolting him out of his reverie, but he ignored it.

A few moments later, the ringing stopped.

Then started again.

Whenever his kids called, they wouldn't give up unless he answered.

Jericho dragged his heavy limbs out of the water, snatched a towel and, wrapping it around his waist, padded barefoot to pick up in the upstairs hall.

'Hello?'

'Dad?'

Cold rivulets of water trickled down his exposed skin. He

towelled himself with one hand. 'How are you, boy?'

'I'm fine. You took your time answering.'

'I was in the bath. The truth is, I almost didn't bother.'

'Why would you say that?'

'It's snowing, boy.'

'What kind of answer is that?'

Jericho shivered. 'I had a drink.'

'You promised me—'

'Had a rough day, son. So what?'

'Want to talk about it?'

Jericho sucked in a breath. 'No.'

Jack hesitated, then said, 'You finish repairing the house?'

'Apart from a final coat of paint, yes.'

'That's great, but you need to get some help next year.'

'No, boy. I like to do it; it keeps my mind off things.'

'Will you come over for Christmas?'

'Alberta mid-winter? No thanks. I'm not going anywhere that's colder than here.'

'Okay, so why not go to Emily?'

'Australia? It's too far. No, son. I stay here; you know that.'

'Yeah, I do,' Jack said. 'One of these days, I'm coming over to drag you back with me kicking and screaming.'

'You'll have to wait until you are man enough—'

'Like when I thrashed you at swing ball when I was seven?'

Jericho paused. 'You remember that?'

'Of course.'

'In the garden?'

'Where else?' Jack laughed. 'I challenged you after winning against Mum and Emily.'

'That's right,' he said. 'But I wasn't sure we got to play that day.'

'Is that another thing you've conveniently forgotten?'

'No, no. The wild-haired highlander who came over—he interrupted us. So, I wasn't sure we actually played, that's all.'

'What wild-haired highlander?'

Jericho exhaled deeply. 'You don't remember?'

'Are you okay?' Jack said.

He hesitated. He'd never confided in anyone about the vivid nightmare he'd had the morning Anita died. All memory of it smothered for years; he wondered if she really had shared with him the horror which played out and if it had indeed killed her. The kids had been in it, too, but neither one had ever talked about it. He always thought they'd suppressed it, just like him. This is insane. How could he raise it as a premonition only now?

'Dad? You still there?'

'I've been thinking about your mum.'

26

'She wouldn't want you drinking.'

'You don't get to lecture me,' Jericho said. 'What do you know, anyway?'

Jack kept his voice even. 'When mum died, you isolated yourself.'

'You wouldn't understand. Too much in the old house reminded me of her and what happened. To move on, I had to leave there.'

'But so far from anywhere? You've made it harder for Emily and me to visit.'

Jericho picked at his memory. Had he consciously kept them away, opting out of family activities because he preferred to be alone? Once, he'd overheard Anita telling the children: *Your father doesn't mix well with other people.* Had he been a drinker even then? 'I've always stood on my own two feet. I need solitude. Not sure I ever should have settled down. I'm a loner, son. Always have been.'

'Nice,' Jack snapped. 'What are you saying? You regret having Emily and me?'

Jericho's voice softened. 'That's not what I meant. Wait a minute, let me get some clothes on.' A slew of thoughts jockeyed for attention as he wandered into the bedroom, the cordless phone clamped to his ear by his shoulder. He took a bottle of whisky from the top drawer of his bedside cabinet. A chasm yawned. The distance between him and his son stretched further as he spun open the cap and swigged. Finally, he spoke. 'The night your mother died....'

Inwardly cursing at the hash he'd made of explaining things to Jack, Jericho returned downstairs and poured a drink. The boy probably thinks I'm crazier than he did before. He placed the tumbler on the small table by his favourite armchair and approached the fire, removing the guard. Already flushed with whisky, his cheeks grew hotter as he stoked the half-charred logs with a poker. He replaced the mesh guard and backed into his chair. Flames reignited, and the scent of birch smoke seeped into his nostrils. Within the contents of his glass, the firelight conjured images of red, orange and yellow. Phantoms from a forgotten past swirled like dervishes behind the lens of its amber playhouse. He stared, mesmerised. Back then, he'd seen himself in the future, living in the house he'd moved to after his wife's death.

Jack didn't get it. Jericho knew what he was trying to say, but couldn't articulate it. He hadn't quite figured it out. A piece of the puzzle was missing. What was it? Unable to hold a sequence of thoughts together for any length of time, he reached into the rack next to his chair. His fingers raked the bottom until he found a pen and withdrew it, along with a crumpled crossword magazine. Leafing through pages of incomplete puzzles, looking for a blank space to write in, he shook his head. When did you finish one of these last? He scratched the ballpoint at the base of a half-empty page. It had dried up. Shit. Too weary to find another, he leaned back and closed his eyes. The wind howled. With a start, he snatched himself from the brink of slumber.

Blizzard-driven snow buffeted the windows, sticking to the glass. An uneasy feeling crept over him. He walked to the gun cabinet and unlocked it, lifting out his shotgun. Shaking ammunition from a box onto the shelf, he scooped a handful of cartridges into his cardigan pocket. His fingers ran over the cold metal as he loaded the breach and carried the gun into the lounge. He leaned forward at the window facing the woods, craning his head left and right before

28

moving to the French doors. Uncannily, like his nightmare, he imagined coming across them open and the wolf slinking through.

Jericho stared at his reflection in the glass. The weapon looked good in his hands. He swung the shotgun barrel up and took aim.

If his long-forgotten dream were a premonition, he hoped it would come true.

Chapter 4

A plume of barbeque smoke billowed into Emily's face. The breeze pursued her as she strode to the opposite side to escape. Tongs in hand, she turned over kebabs before switching tools and flipping burgers. Shit, they're overdone. She half-smiled. Her cooking was a standing joke. Once, when she surpassed herself, the meal almost perfect, her best friend had remarked, 'There's something wrong with this grub.'

'What's that?' Emily asked.

'It's not *burnt,*' Celine said, bursting into laughter.

Kurt and his friends wouldn't even notice. Emily grinned at him. He saluted her with a can of beer.

Australia. Such a big step at the time. Now, Emily couldn't envisage being anywhere else. She imagined her father living in the Scottish wilderness. When he'd announced his new address, the first thing she did was google it. Her dad now lived in an area once plagued by cannibals. Granted, that was five hundred years ago, but no way she could ever live there. And Jack. Inseparable once, if Mum were still alive, neither of them would ever have left England. 'Don't give me a second thought,' Jericho said.

Reluctant at first, she conceded he'd steered her into happiness beyond her dreams.

'You're burning the bloody prawns.' Kurt yelled.

Emily hurriedly flipped the food on the grill. 'Just making sure it's cooked properly.'

The outside telephone bell rattled, the sound muted.

'Phone, Ems.' Kurt's hand mimed a receiver and wiggled it by his ear.

'I never heard it.' Emily said, pointing to the metal ringer on the wall. 'You'd best look at that. I reckon something's built a nest in it.' She wiped her hands on a tea cloth, reached inside the open patio doors and lifted the handset.

She looked at the caller's name on display and grinned. 'Hi, this is Emily. I can't pick up your call right now,' she said, in an answerphone voice. 'But if—'

Jack laughed. 'Okay, okay. You had me going for a moment. Are you having a party?'

'Just a barbie for a few friends.' Raucous laughter erupted in the background. Emily slid the door closed. 'You okay, little brother?'

'I'm fine.' He cleared his throat. 'Oh, before I forget. You owe me for the Death Anniversary Notice.'

'I paid last time, bloody cheek.'

'This one I put in The Times, so it's extra, but don't worry. Ten years without Mum. Can you believe it?'

'No, I bloody can't,' she said.

'I phoned Dad today.'

'How is he?'

'I'm worried about him,' Jack said.

31

'He can take care of himself.'

'Yeah… It's just—he was so drunk. Told me he'd been thinking about Mum.'

'Today of all days, you'd expect it,' Emily sighed. 'At least he remembers her. I'll call him.'

'Has he ever spoken to you about the night she died?'

'Only that Mum had had a heart attack, and he couldn't do anything to save her.'

'Well, he had more to say about it earlier.'

'Like what?'

'It was strange. Made no sense at all. Talking about a wolf coming after them in a dream.' Jack took a deep breath. 'According to him, that was the actual cause of her coronary…Do you remember how old we were when Mum died?'

'Are you serious? I was twenty-seven.'

'That's what I mean. Dad couldn't recall. When I told him, he started doing mental arithmetic and rambling about how we'd all been at his house in Scotland years ago before he even owned it. Then he ran through this nightmare. Asked if I remembered being there and whether you'd ever mentioned it? In short, he thinks it was real. A premonition. It's the first time I've heard any of this.'

'Same here,' Emily said. 'It was the drink talking; you know how he gets.'

'I'm not sure I do anymore,' Jack said and fell silent.

'You still there?' Emily said.

'Yes, sorry. Just thinking. Chantelle is reading this book

32

about the effects of trauma. I think he's suffering from undiagnosed post-traumatic stress disorder.'

'Mum always thought that, and she tried to get him into therapy, but you know how that ended. He went ballistic.' She paused at a burst of laughter from her guests and peeked through the blinds. 'I just don't know....'

'Well, what else could it be?'

'He's lonely?' Emily said.

'Is that a statement or a question? It's hard to tell since you moved down under.'

Emily laughed. 'Little brother, you're a brat.'

'Christ, why did we listen to him and move so far away?'

'Because he made it seem like such a good idea.' A hum of low, conspiratorial tones drew her attention. She moved closer to the door.

'I invited him for Christmas.'

'You wasted your breath, Jack.'

'I had to ask.'

'Of course,' Emily said. 'I've lost count of the times I've asked him over... stay a few months, but he won't do it.'

'Come springtime, I'll visit him. Can't take a vacation before that.'

'You don't get it, do you? He wants to be alone. I'll call him later. He'll be fine.'

'Let me know what he says.'

'Oh God, something's burning,' she said. 'Got to go. I'll chat with you tomorrow?'

'Bye, sis.'

Emily hung the phone back in its cradle, slid open the doors and, shielding her eyes from the sun, rushed to the smoke-shrouded barbeque.

Chapter 5

Jericho turned off all the downstairs lights and, shotgun cradled in his arms, patrolled the darkened rooms, looking out into the night from each window. The whisky hadn't brought him solace. Tonight, fear, anger and disappointment, combined with the rising storm, left his nerves frayed.

Jack's right, he'd given his word, and now it was what? Two drinks, three or five? Unsure, he crossed the quarry-tiled floor in the hall and turned into the kitchen to check the bottle. Half-empty. He walked into the lounge. Long flames flickered in the hearth, creating silhouettes that danced around the room like refugee puppets from a shadow theatre.

The fire drew in him. In the mirror over the mantle, his underlit face appeared red-tinged and demonic. Try as he might, he couldn't shake Jack's earlier denials.

'You don't know that, Dad! You might believe it—'

'Son, you weren't there. You never lived it—'

'Neither did you! It was a nightmare, for God's sake.'

'You think I'm crazy, is that it?'

'Of course not, but how do you forget something as profound as that for ten years and only just remember it now? You bottled up your feelings, and they're leeching out. This is you dealing with what you didn't face back then. She had a massive heart attack. Even if you'd been a doctor, you couldn't have done a thing. Mum was beyond saving.'

Doubt burrowed into him like a worm.

No, the boy's wrong.

Jericho knew he had to get them away. Why else did he fund their journeys? Set them up with new beginnings. It thrilled him when he learned they'd met prospective partners from far-flung lands. They were safe. If he had understood back then what really happened to Anita and he'd done all of that, how could he have forgotten?

He leant in close, staring into the mirror, into the black depths of his pupils, as empty as the glass left by the chair. When had he downed the contents?

Jack's right. I'm losing it. How many years have I wasted in a wilderness of my own making? Well, no more. Tears surprised him and ran in rivulets down his cheeks. 'If the invite still holds,' he whispered. 'I'm coming over for Christmas, boy, and on to Emily's in the New Year... if she'll have me.'

He relaxed his grip, laid down the weapon, and squinted at his wristwatch. 8:35 pm. Years of mentally calculating the difference between their respective time zones told him it was too early to ring his daughter in Melbourne. All right, Jack first. Now, where did I leave the phone? He started for the stairs and then stopped. With frightening acceleration, the wind rose through the scales. Deep flute sounds from the chimney reached a crescendo. The god of the wild was calling the tune.

Driving snow blanketed the northward-facing windows. Unable to see, Jericho rushed to peer through the French doors on the east side. Lit by moonlight, a machine-gun blur of white tracer bullets filled the air. Nothing could survive out there for long. His ears tuned into creaking timbers everywhere. No force of nature had struck his home like this before. The floor quaked beneath his feet.

The house is mainly timber. Could it blow away? Had the Three Little Pigs been a fairy tale inspired by a storm or the fear of a stalking wolf? Was this how the story originated? Isn't this how all fairy stories came about, and aren't they a way of warning us that the world is never quite what it seems?

Suddenly, the logs in the grate popped and fizzed. Puzzled, Jericho crouched, ducked under the nook of the fireplace, and looked up into the dark void. Water dripped, dowsing the flames, but how could it get down the chimney? In the morning, he'd check the weathering cowl hadn't blown away.

Something thudded into the house. Startled, he jerked upright and then, in a flurry of fluid motion, he commando-rolled, jumped to his feet, and launched himself for the gun, snatching it up by the barrel.

His head cleared. The impact was against the north wall. No good trying to look out of those windows. Jericho dashed for the front door, flipped on the outside lights and prised the letter flap open. Eyes little more than slits, he scanned left and right, blinking off the stinging assault of the blinding snow.

There! Ten yards from the house, barely visible in the halogen lights, a bundle wrapped in white rags. A faint cry carried on the wind.

A child?

No. Bigger than that.

His grip tightened on the shotgun as he focused on the blurred shape; the contours gradually recognised. It's a bird, and a big one. A keen ornithologist, he knew it wasn't native to these parts. The storm had blown it off course. Because of its size, it could only be a crane. He'd heard sometimes they strayed as far north as Scotland. From the sound of the crash, it was unlikely the bird had survived. Even if it were alive, he'd learned from bitter experience the odds of nursing an injured bird back to health were slim. In moments, snow would cover the stricken creature. It's only a stupid bird. Why put it through the stress of being handled when it will perish either way? With sadness in his heart, he slowly lowered the flap.

A call, shrill and one of distress, whistled through the closing gap. Jericho peered outside again.

The gale eased.

He opened the door.

The crane lifted its head from the snowdrift and, for an instant, met his gaze.

Behind the bird, twenty-five yards distant, a large dark shape emerged from the swirling snow; its ice-grey eyes glowered at him, burning with familiar hatred.

Dry-mouthed and with a pounding heart, he slammed the door.

Chapter 6

Jericho slumped against the wall, breathing hard. The urge to dash out, shotgun blazing, was tough to resist. Here it is. Revenge. Got to think. His hands shook. He balled his fists and clenched his jaw. A battle raged inside him; the fusion of alcohol, adrenaline and willpower forced him into instant sobriety and left him rubber-legged and strangely disoriented. One shot. How quickly can he reload? Three seconds. In his current state, maybe five. One shot. Wait for him to come right up. Shoot it, point blank. Kill the fucker outright. Different scenes played out in his mind. A movie in his head started when he stepped outside. Let it come. Let it think it has me. Then, at the last moment, jam the barrel into its teeth, smashing them. Look into the evil fucker's face as I pull the trigger.

The clock ticking in the hall seemed amplified, the silence between beats prolonged.

Anita's voice rose from the depths of his subconscious. Jerry, you're not as sharp as you used to be. If you mess up, what happens to the crane?

'Neet, it's only a bird.'

You can't let the wolf take her.

Crushed, Jericho remembered how he'd done nothing to save his wife. He imagined the wolf bounding through the snow towards the hapless creature, sinking his teeth into its neck, dragging it away in a trail of blood while spindly legs thrashed in the throes of death.

Anita scolded him. *You can't just leave it like that. Please save her. There's no time to lose.*

'You're right,' he said. Clutching the weapon to his chest, he took a long breath, swung around, and threw open the door.

Arctic winds blasted him with hail, stinging his face and eyes. He blinked. A deep snowdrift blocked his way. Cold and damp already seeping into his clothes, he waded knee-high into the snow and squinted through the blur of falling flakes, the grounds, an undulating white moonscape. Shotgun raised, he sighted along its length, sweeping left and right. No dark shadow moving in, no visible trail.

'Where are you?' Jericho said, filled with apprehension, knowing he couldn't show fear. Predators sense it.

'Come on,' he shouted, beating his chest. 'I know you're out there.'

The bird shuffled, raised its head, and turned towards him, beak parted, silent.

Pink eyes. Albino. Something triggered in him. Flaming torches. African drums. Fierce bonfires. A procession weaving past villages and hills... 'No,' Jericho said and shook the images away.

Savage gusts roared, rippling the snow. Loose particles swept from the surface and swirled into wraith-like forms, unnerving him. *This creature is no snaw ghast. It is a demon.* Fillan's warning loomed in the back of his mind.

Ten paces from the fallen bird, finger tight on the trigger, Jericho searched the terrain and ploughed onwards.

As a man of the world, he knew wolves hunted and feasted on carrion only when starvation left them no alternative. It could've dragged the crane away before I came out. Why didn't it? Is the fucker using it as bait?

Senses heightened, he stood on tiptoes to better see. Still, he saw no tracks. He focused on the low shrubs scattered across the front garden. A grim smile cracked his lips. 'You think I don't know your game?' he yelled. 'That I don't know who you are?'

Soaked through, his cardigan pockets sagged under the weight of his cartridges. One shot. I can't afford to miss it.

Snow crusted Jericho's trousers below the knee, damp and cold against his shins. Unable to feel his toes, he stamped his feet, removed his right hand from the gun, blew into his cupped fist and flexed his frozen trigger finger.

A white mound erupted from the ground ten yards away and charged towards him, kicking up spray. Snow fell in clumps, revealing matted black fur.

Bracing himself, Jericho levelled the weapon, aiming. 'You cunning bastard,' he snarled. The crane lay directly in the line of fire. There was no way he could shoot without hitting it.

The beast slowed down, looking from man to bird and back again. It stalked closer, keeping the bird between them. With a wicked gleam in its eye, it locked him in its gaze and squatted within pouncing distance, issuing a silent challenge.

It's not scared, not how it should be. 'You think I won't shoot?' He took a step nearer to help negate the chances of hitting the stricken crane. 'You think you can play with me?'

As he got closer to the bird, he saw it was bigger than he'd imagined. He didn't know how much it weighed, but it had to be five feet long from head to toe. He couldn't just slip it under his arm and dash for the cottage. Nor could he carry it and aim his gun, let alone shoot. The cold stinging his face, he considered his options.

Jericho crept closer, his gaze locked on the beast's drooling jaws. The air between them misted with vaporous breath.

'Oh, I know what you're thinking. I can't leave the bird, or it'll die of cold. You think I'll put the gun down to save it? That's when you'll make your move?'

The wolf sank deeper into its haunches, a deep growl rumbling in its throat, lips drawn taut against jagged yellow teeth, steely grey eyes filled with menace.

'Do you think you can trick me into wasting a shot?' His hand slid up the polished wooden stock. A new plan dawned on him. 'Well, not tonight, fucker.'

Jericho inched forward and knelt while keeping the gun pointed at the wolf. The crane scooped so it nestled against his chest as he stood. His finger tight on the trigger, he crab-walked back to the house.

The wolf snarled and slunk into the open, head down. Not taking its eyes off the man or bird, it weaved from side to side, stalking him.

The bundle he carried was now his responsibility, and knowing the blast could give the bird a heart attack, he resisted the urge to shoot.

He tripped over a hidden obstruction beneath the snow and fell to the side. The crane slid down along the polished gunmetal; he dropped to a knee and teetered on the verge of overbalancing.

The predator reacted immediately.

Three swift, bounding leaps. Another, and it would seize him. Adrenaline surged in his veins. Jericho's perception of time slowed. He altered his grip, somehow keeping hold of the injured bird, and shifted the helpless creature closer to his breast, the wolf close enough to smell. Heart pounding in his ears, he raised the gun barrel, every fibre screaming, *shoot!*

He squeezed the trigger. *Boom!*

Taken mid-stride, the wolf tumbled to one side, rolled over, and got back to its feet. Blood dripping from its fur, it turned around, eyes blazing with hatred, and then charged, throwing up a white cascade of frost which, whipped by the wind, drove into him like icy nails.

Impossible. I shot it point blank. He fled to the house, elbowed the handle down, backed in, and kicked the door shut.

The wolf slammed into the door as he bolted it. Putting down the gun, he eased the limp bird into his hands, relieved to feel warm skin through its soft plumage. It'll be a miracle if you survive.

Outside, the beast growled, tearing at the wooden door frame.

'I'll rip your heart out,' he yelled.

An ominous silence followed.

Autopilot took over, and he carried the motionless crane into the lounge. 'I need to get you warm.' In the fire's glow, he laid the bird on the hearth and went to change his wet clothes.

Passing the lobby, he wrinkled his nose. What's that smell? A rancid stench blew through the door. Jesus, it's piss.

The bastard just scent-marked the house.

Chapter 7

Jack sat at the dining table, hunched over a laptop, scrolling the mouse wheel as he read the screen.

Cold hands covered his eyes from behind. '*Devine qui?* Guess who?'

Her voice never failed to put a smile on his face. 'My favourite French woman? If not, you'd better leave before Chantelle gets here.' He swivelled in his chair to face her. 'Still snowing?'

She stepped back and flicked her lush dark hair, spraying him with droplets of melted snow. 'What are you doing?'

'Just looking up stuff.'

'Don't let me stop you.' She slipped an arm around his shoulder and manoeuvred herself onto his lap. 'I bought some things I want to show you.'

'Let me finish, babe,' he said.

'What's so important that your immediate attention is not on me?' She gave him a mock-serious look and switched her focus to the screen. 'Why are you looking for the Day of the Dead?'

'Just something my dad mentioned when I called him earlier. It's also known as All Souls' Day.'

Her finger traced a line in the article. 'Says here,

November 2nd. That's today, non?'

'Yeah.'

'How is he?'

'It's the anniversary of Mum's death.'

'Oh, chéri.' She leaned away to better see his face. 'I'm sorry.'

'I think he's given up on life,' he said. His eyes misted. 'He just wasn't making sense. He's drunk. Got himself in a state. Anyway, he was rattling on about this strange Scotsman telling him that if snow fell today, this wolf would appear.'

'What wolf?'

'Baby, I don't know.'

She hugged him. 'It is a Mexican celebration, non? Is it a thing in Scotland?'

'No idea,' he said. 'You interrupted me before I finished researching.'

She arched an eyebrow. 'Let's look at this together,' she said and keyed in a new search string.

Jack studied the results. 'Seems that the Scots don't call it that. It doesn't really matter. It was just him rambling about nightmares and warnings.'

'What sort of warnings, chéri?'

He sighed. 'We're giving this a credibility that isn't warranted. You don't know him like I do. It's paranoia. Whisky talk.'

'C'mon.' Chantelle shifted from his lap and pulled

another chair up beside him. 'Indulge me.'

'He said this guy approached him while we were playing in the garden.' Jack took his glasses off to rub his eyes. 'I'm not sure about this.'

She grinned sympathetically. 'C'mon, don't be embarrassed.'

Jack half-smiled. 'He asked if I remembered playing swing ball in the garden with Emily and Mum when I was seven and then challenging him to a game?'

'From the look on your face, you don't recall it?'

'Well, funnily enough, I do. It's just that he related it as if it were the evening before Mum died, and it couldn't have been. I was twenty-five when she passed. Then he told me someone killed Scotland's last wolf in the 1700s, but another one appeared forty years later.' His shoulders slumped. 'He's lost it, baby.'

Chantelle stood, placed a hand on his head and ruffled his hair. 'Did you check it out?'

'The wolf business? No.'

'Google it.'

'Chantelle,' he forced a smile. 'It's enough.'

She reached over and typed *The Last Wolf in Scotland* into the search box. Wikipedia topped the list. They studied the page.

He watched her eyes follow the text on the screen.

'Wow,' she said. 'Scottish wolves were more dangerous than their English cousins. See here: *Once considered such a threat, the authorities built special houses to shelter travellers from wolf attacks.*'

Jack leaned closer to the monitor. 'It also says official records state the last one died in 1680.'

'Yes, and two lines down, it says 1743.'

'Strangely enough, Dad mentioned that date. Oh, see there? It says folklore.'

'There's another sighting in 1888!'

'Babe,' he said. 'It's unconfirmed,'

'No smoke without the fire,' she retorted.

'And the stranger talking about the Day of the Dead? That's an unusual term in Scotland?'

'Right. Let's look at that.'

Jack squeezed her playfully. 'You're like a little dog with a bone.'

Chantelle brushed his hand away. 'Now, let's see…' She typed *Day of the Dead or All Souls' Day in Scotland* and hit return. 'Here's something. New festival to create a Scottish Day of the Dead in the Mexican tradition.' Her voice trailed as she completed the preview. 'It's nothing relevant, after all.'

'What's this?' He pointed to a line further down. *To Absent Friends: A People's Festival of Storytelling and Remembrance?* 'Dad always raises a glass to absent friends.'

'That doesn't explain why a Scot would use a Mexican term. Let's try this.' Fingers flashed across the keys, followed by the enter tab.

'The Scottish in Mexico?' Jack grinned at the results. 'Wow! That's got you all of four names.'

'Are you mocking me, Mr Mathers?'

He held up his hands in mock surrender. 'I wouldn't dare. Come on, let's go to bed.'

Ignoring him, she said, 'Mmm, looks like the earliest mention was in the nineteenth century.' She rattled off another search. 'Look at this. "In 1556, the English adventurer Robert Thomson encountered a Scotsman, Thomas Blake, who had been living in Mexico City for over twenty years."'

'You place a lot of reliance on Wikipedia, baby. And you're using it to concoct supporting evidence for the direction you'd like the narrative to go.'

'Am I? Doesn't it make sense that if people migrated there, they might eventually return, possibly bringing with them traditions from another land?'

He shrugged the French way. 'Yes?'

'Your mom died on All Souls' Day?'

'I never realised it until now, but what of it?'

She clicked the back button on the browser three times. 'Right here, it says the dead can visit their loved ones on All Souls' Night.'

'It's a myth,' he said, shaking his head. 'If you believe that, you're as crazy as he is.'

'You need to talk to your father. Call him again.'

Whisking her off her feet and into a fireman's lift, he said, 'I will, but later.'

Chapter 8

The crane hadn't moved since Jericho laid it by the hearth. Fiery hues of red and gold licked the bird's white feathers, lending them an illusion of animation. Awed by its beauty, he crept closer, his gaze fixed on the prone form. Reaching out, he stroked its long, soft neck. 'I couldn't save my wife when the wolf came before, so the least I can do now is to ensure you survive. Although I have to say my record isn't a good one.' He pictured himself solemn-eyed as a child, holding a sealed cardboard box while his father dug a grave for a blackbird they'd rescued from a cat. The bird lived less than twenty-four hours.

Satisfied he'd done all he could, he retrieved the shotgun and strode down the hallway. At the foot of the stairs, he grasped the top of the newel post and hesitated.

A voice from a distant time floated into his consciousness.

It's all right. Daddy's calling the police.

'I let you down, didn't I? And even after all these years, I haven't learned a thing.' His eyes pricked, and he swallowed hard. 'Jesus, what I would give for another chance?'

His fingers felt for the light switch and turned it on, taking the steps two at a time. Once on the landing, he put the gun down, stripped off his wet clothes, and left them in a heap outside the bathroom.

Jericho opened the airing cupboard, grabbed a towel, dried his hair and beard, and rubbed himself down before marching to his bedroom.

What to wear? With his wardrobe doors flung open, he dressed quickly based on practicality. He retrieved the phone from its charger, grabbed the weapon with his free hand, and returned downstairs. In the lounge, he switched on the light and dialled 999. 'Come on, come on, answer,' he muttered. It occurred to him he'd have to ask them to send a sharpshooter, but he knew no one would attend until the blizzard cleared. Same with the vet, but at least they could advise him on bird care.

'No reply. Some emergency service this is!'

A movement by the hearth caught his eye.

'Did you just move?' With the handset still against his ear, he edged closer. Imperceptibly, the clawed feet flexed and curled inwards as if clutching an invisible rock. Rigor mortis? Gentle fingers probing, he felt her breast. There's a heartbeat. He smiled. 'I don't have a box big enough to fit you in. The best I can do is cover your head with a cloth so you don't panic when you wake up.'

Jericho turned and reached for an old blanket he'd used to cover a hole in the leather armchair by the window. Outside, a dark blur shot past. On his feet in an instant, he pressed his face against the cold glass. 'Is that you, you devil?' he whispered.

The temperature dropped in direct proportion to the pitch of the screeching wind. Lights flickered and died, including his phone. Gooseflesh crawled over his clammy skin. His senses tingled. Time slowed. He cocked his head. What *is* that noise? It matched one that he was all too familiar with. The back door handle.

51

Jericho snatched up his shotgun and rushed along the darkened hall, almost crashing into the wall as he swept around the corner into the back room.

On its hind legs, the wolf glowered at him through the French doors, pawing at the lever handle, jiggling it up and down.

He raised his weapon and aimed. Finger hovering on the trigger, he pondered on the lead pellets blasting through the pane and losing their velocity. What if he didn't kill the beast with a single shot? It hadn't worked before. What if it used the resultant shattered pane to force its way in? He lowered the gun.

The wolf snarled, dropped to all fours, and cocked his leg sideways. A jet of urine splattered on the glass.

'I'll kill you,' he roared. 'You hear me?'

Without a hint of concern, the creature loped out of sight.

The bastard's circling the house.

Where's my mobile?

Jericho dashed to the kitchen and grabbed the phone to try the emergency services again when he noticed the message on the signal bar. No network. Try upstairs. The coverage is always better.

On the first-floor landing, he held the phone aloft, his eyes focused on the screen. Still nothing, so he paced from room to room. The lack of signal remained unchanged. Thoughts racing, he visualised his car outside. Even if he had made it, the roads would have been impassable, making rescue impossible until the storm had passed.

Christ, we're trapped!

Chapter 9

Chantelle slowly extricated herself from Jack's embrace and sat up. She checked the bedside clock.

'Mon Dieu, chéri, wake up.' She nudged him. 'You must call your father.'

He groaned and opened one eye. 'What's the time?'

'15:33,' she said.

'It's too late.'

'In Scotland, it is 22:30, non? He will not be sleeping yet.'

'Baby, I don't want to hear his drunken voice.'

'Fine. Don't talk. Just say you called to wish him good night.'

'Are you kidding?' he said. 'He'll think I've gone soft. Besides, I haven't said that to him since I was a kid.'

'Say it now.' Chantelle leaned over him. 'He needs to feel you.'

His mouth sought hers.

She giggled, twisted away, and placed the phone in his hand. 'Do it.'

'He won't answer.'

'Then you have nothing to lose.'

'Okay, okay,' he said, and dialling the number, put the phone to his ear. After a few moments, he frowned.

She raised her eyebrows. 'Non?'

'Can't get through. There's a disconnected service tone.'

'Try his cell.'

'Okay,' he said, selecting his dad's saved number. A pre-recorded operator message cut in: *It has not been possible to connect your call.*

Chantelle registered mild concern in her husband's eyes. She rose and padded naked to the laptop in the dining room; smoothing her hair, she ducked to check her reflection in the black monitor. Bending over, she tapped the mouse. The screen lit up. Finger at the ready, she guided the cursor into the Google search box and, typed, *report telephone fault, Scotland* and clicked the icon. None of the options looked promising. Although now that she'd established BT as the service provider, she accessed their website.

'What are you doing, babe?'

'Looking at a map of telephone outages in your father's region.'

'What's it say?'

'Wow! The entire area is down.'

'Does it say why?' he said. 'Let me see.'

Chantelle moved aside to make room for him at the table.

'In the forum, customers say freak weather in the north of Scotland caused it.'

'High winds?'

'Blizzards too,' she said, scrolling the page. 'Look at all the posts about cars skidding off highways.'

'Well, that won't affect Dad too much—'

'Precisely, unless he is on the roads?'

'No, there's no reason he'd be out.'

'Here, this witness saw a lorry taking out power and telephone lines in a single accident.'

'That means he'll be unreachable for days. A bit of snow and everything stops. They can't cope the way they do everywhere else in Europe.'

'His cell signal will return as soon as the storm breaks.'

Jack shrugged and drew up a chair. 'Weather like that is unheard of this early in Scotland. It could go on for weeks.'

Chantelle swivelled to face him. 'Tell me, did you and your father discuss anything else?'

'I can't remember.'

'Look at me. I've only met your father once, and I am curious to find out how similar you are.'

'We aren't alike.'

'You are both stubborn.'

Jack met her gaze. 'Maybe.'

'Not maybe,' she said, grinning. 'You are!'

'Did I tell you he's learning French?'

She clapped her hands and smiled gleefully. 'When was this?'

A sheepish look crossed his face.

'How long ago, chéri?'

'I told you last month.'

'You did not.'

'Sure I did. Dad said he'd been thinking about it ever since our wedding. Doesn't think he'll find it hard, especially as he already speaks Gaelic.'

'He does?'

'Yes, he buried himself in studying the language after Mum died.'

'I imagine it helped him cope, but you did not tell me any of this before?' Chantelle arched an eyebrow. 'Do not say you did because I forget nothing.'

'Babe, I'm sorry. This new job's a hassle—'

Her finger pressed against his lips. 'Scotland and France have a long history. I'm certain there are many similarities between our languages. You know,' she said. 'If your father is learning le Français, he has not given up on life.'

'Sure, but you didn't speak to him.'

'As soon as the weather breaks, you must call. We should visit. I can't wait to converse with my father-in-law, *en Français!*'

Jack's hand folded over hers. 'I'd like nothing more, but it's a no-go until after my appraisal finishes at the end of February.'

'That's too long to wait. If we cannot go to Scotland, then your father... he must come to us.'

Chapter 10

Jericho checked the signal on his mobile. It remained at zero. The battery level remaining was less than half. It could be enough for another twelve hours, but what if the power didn't come back on? Setting the phone to low-power mode, he crossed the lounge, squatted by the dwindling fire, and peeled back the blanket covering the crane. He lay down alongside the bird. Propped on an elbow, he examined the stricken creature. In the same way chicken sexers determine male and female chicks, he just knew she was female. *Please save her...* he realised Anita had known it, too.

His upper body slumped until his cheek touched her beak. *She's not breathing.* His fingertips felt for a heartbeat in the downy depths of her breast. Her pulse was weak.

With a grim smile on his face, he whispered, 'Hang in there. When you wake, I'll see if I can get you to take some water.'

He stood, drew the blanket back over her and noted the time: 10:37 pm. A candle flickered in the kitchen, drawing his gaze to the whisky bottle framed in the serving hatch. Moistening his lips, he said, 'This is going to be a long night.'

Jericho moved the fire guard and stoked the dying embers, teasing a short-lived burst of radiance from them. Satisfied the timbers had burned beyond their capacity to spit, he didn't replace the guard, knowing he needed more logs. He slid the crane closer to the warmth and lifted her onto the hearth. Against the cool terracotta tiles, he felt something wet on his fingers. In the half-light, a crescent-shaped brown and white smear gleamed at him.

'Nothing wrong with that end of you,' he said, wiping his hand clean on a tissue. 'I rarely talk to myself, you know. At least, I don't think I do? Listen, Bird, I've got to get more logs, or we'll freeze to death.'

To step outside in a blizzard without locating the wolf was suicidal. The snow-covered windows prevented him from seeing where it was. He chewed his lower lip, thinking it through. I could use the chairs from the dining room as fuel. That would buy us a couple of hours, but then I'll be out there, anyway. He abandoned the idea.

'I might get to the shed unscathed, Birdy, but how do I make it back carrying a sack full of logs?' Jericho stroked his beard. 'There's rope out there. If I tie it to a sack filled with wood, I can hold the wolf at bay with the shotgun in one hand and run, taking up the slack in the other until I'm at the front door. Then I'll haul it over. It'll be hard, but it's workable.'

He ducked and looked through the letterbox, eyes straining for a dark shape slinking through the snow, but saw nothing.

'We're in the lap of the gods. I couldn't save my wife, but I'll do my utmost to keep you alive. Where that wolf's hiding, I don't know but fuck it. If we're to live, this needs doing.'

Jericho stomped down the corridor, snatched his trench coat from a hook in the hall, selected a long scarf from an adjacent peg, and wrapped it three times around his throat like a samurai bandaging his abdomen. Next, he put on his hiking boots. Shotgun in hand, he strode into the kitchen, picked up a butcher's knife and tucked it into his belt.

Back at the door, he checked outside again. Still nothing.

Taking a deep breath, he drew back the bolts.

Something made him stop. Through the letterbox, he strained to see into the blind spot where the north and eastern walls met opposite the wood store.

In the shadows, camouflaged by snow and barely discernible, the wolf crouched, facing the shed, its back to him, watching and waiting.

Jericho paced the room. The fucker! How does it know? The furrow in his brow deepened. The flicker of candlelight from the kitchen cast a sense of unreality over the situation. Scent. That's it! Front door, rear door. The woodshed. All the places he frequented most. The wolf had worked it out using a simple process of elimination. Nothing supernatural about that, but then he realised why it had staked out the shed. It knew he would need fuel.

Had it invaded his consciousness all those years ago and lain dormant, waiting for the snow to fall on All Souls Day?

Could it read his mind?

Despite his overcoat and scarf, Jericho shivered. No doubt about it, this evil had to be destroyed, come what may, but how? It seemed conventional means wouldn't work. Still, he'd drawn blood. Therefore, it was vulnerable.

With the wind in his favour, he'd slip out the back door and creep up on it from behind. No, it'll hear that damned creak as soon as he opens it.

There must be another way.

Scene after scene played out in his thoughts. In each, he emerged the victor, albeit every triumph was flawed. *Glory-seeking clouds your judgement; you romanticise the outcome.* Who in his past had said that?

The car. It's closer to the house than the shed. At first, the wolf will hear me come out. That's what he's expecting, and he'll think I'm walking into his ambush.

What if it can read your mind, Jerry?

Could he disguise his thoughts by concentrating on Anita? It had to be worth a shot.

A fresh buzz of adrenaline surged through him. Jericho washed his face in cold water, carefully drying it. The act of cleansing chased the last vestiges of alcohol from his veins, sharpening his senses. His heart thumped out a staccato beat, and his eardrums pumped along to the same rhythm. He grabbed the car keys, cocked his gun, and checked the knife in his belt. Ready.

Satisfied the wolf hadn't left its hideaway, he opened the front door and stepped outside, fighting the gale to pull it silently shut behind him.

Freezing air and snow blasted him. His face pinched against the cold, he hunched deep into his scarf.

A dozen paces away, completely entombed, his four-wheel-drive awaited.

With the ever-present whistling of the wind climbing the scales into a mournful wail, he pressed the remote button. *Beep-beep.* The headlights came on. Jericho shoved the keys into his pocket and waded towards the vehicle. Alerted by peripheral movement, he swung around. Clouds of snow puffed into the air, obscuring the dark shape ploughing through the frozen surface towards him.

His testicles shrank into his body as he waded ahead, arms aloft, using the gun to aid his balance.

Every leap drew the wolf closer.

Turn. Shoot. Jericho faltered. What if it doesn't stop it? I might not make it to the vehicle if I waste crucial seconds. His thoughts turned to Jack and Emily. The chance to visit them over Christmas. To save Birdy. Do Anita proud. On leaden legs, he pushed on.

At the car, he scythed snow from it with the stock of his shotgun, probing the thick residue, and searched for the handle.

He glanced over his shoulder. The wolf, intent and now just yards from him, leapt closer.

Fingers hooked under the lever, Jericho jerked upward and pulled. Shit! Frozen. He dropped the gun and yanked with both hands, to no avail. The point of his knife jammed between the door and bodywork; he prised while pulling the handle. 'Give, dammit,' he yelled.

The distance between them halved; he gauged the wolf's next leap.

'Come on!' Desperate, he slammed his shoulder into the bodywork and tried again. It opened. Powdered snow peppered him; he glanced up. The wolf was now two feet away.

My gun! No time. Leave it! Jericho threw himself inside, banging the door shut. The beast's head smacked into the window, jaws gnashing a zig-zag trail of saliva down the glass before disappearing.

Jericho banged his fist against the door. 'Get outta here!' Insulated under thick snow, the vehicle was deathly quiet. He listened for the wolf and heard nothing.

He put the knife on the passenger seat and fished the ignition key from his pocket. The engine started, chugged, misfired, and then caught. He switched on the heated front and rear windscreens and set the thermostat on the blowers to the highest level. Can't turn on the wipers yet. The weight and thickness of snow on top of them could burn out the motor if activated too soon.

The fuel gauge showed a quarter tank. Insufficient to drive for help, and in these conditions, he'd be lucky to make it off his property.

A heavy layer of snow blocked the nearside window; he couldn't see a thing, but if he could align the passenger door with that of the wood store and get close enough to wind the window down safely, he'd climb through and fill the car with sacks of timber.

Jericho revved the engine and allowed it to idle once more. The snow over the windscreen turned greyish, still too heavy for the blades to move. This is taking too long.

Satisfied the wipers could now pass within the melted zone, he turned them on. They laboured up to the twelve o'clock position and halted. He switched them off and slammed both hands onto the steering wheel. 'Fuck!'

Thunk! Suddenly, the car rocked from side to side.

Jericho jumped. What the–?

Claws raked across the glass, setting him on edge as it tried to break in, face pushed into the encrusted snow, bared teeth clacking against the windscreen.

He stared into its eyes, snatched up his knife, and brandished it. 'Fuck off! Do you hear me?'

The wipers, kick-started by the creature's efforts, continued their upward sweep before returning to the start position.

'Keep it up, you dumb fuck.'

It clawed at the windshield relentlessly.

'There I was, giving you credit for intelligence. Now, look at you.' He gazed out through the half-cleared glass. 'You're actually helping me.'

Jericho put the automatic gearshift into drive and applied gentle pressure on the accelerator. The beast continued attacking, unfazed. Tyres crunching, the car inched forward.

'No way you're getting in here.' He knew stamping on the brakes would do little to dislodge his adversary at only three miles per hour. With ten feet to go, he detected the wheels slipping. The heaped snow had created a resistance far greater than the grip of his tyres. Reversing a few yards, he squeezed the accelerator pedal and then shifted the lever into second gear. The pointer on the speedometer touched five miles an hour. He slammed into the pile of snow. The wolf scrambled to stay on board, its claws digging into the head of the screen. A length of metal trim popped out and hung from the rubber windscreen.

Again, he placed the car in reverse, putting an arm across the passenger seat, and drove swiftly backwards. The creature glowered at him from the bonnet as he prepared to go forward again. Defiant, he returned the beast's stare. Then, wheels spinning, he launched into the accumulation of snow again. Faster than his previous attempt, the car collided with the heap. Thrown backwards, it bit down, tearing loose the piece of trim as it vanished from view.

Precariously close, he couldn't risk another run-up without knocking into the outbuildings. Just a couple more feet. Again, he edged backwards and shunted forwards. Another foot gained. Eighteen inches further, and he'd have the shed and car doors perfectly aligned. One more time. He repeated the process a little faster than intended. The car slewed into the wood store. It creaked under the load the vehicle brought to bear on it.

Jericho checked the alignment of the two doors. Not perfect, but it was the best he'd get.

Alert for danger, he switched on the interior light and pressed the electric window button. An icy blast of air hit him. He shuffled across the passenger seat, picking up the knife as he did so. Satisfied the gap between the building and the car was too narrow for the wolf, he leaned from the opening and used the blade to unlatch the door. It swung inwards. He hesitated. Go out headfirst? Not a good idea. His legs swung up from the footwell, and pivoting on the seat, he rested his body weight on his elbows and thrust both feet outside. Two hands were required to complete the contortion, so he clenched the weapon between his teeth. Legs dangling, he rolled onto his front and wriggled backwards into the gloom of the store.

Not yet accustomed to the darkness, he removed the knife from his mouth and carefully tucked it into his belt. He squeezed his eyes shut and held them closed for ten seconds. When he reopened them, his visibility had improved sufficiently to locate the log-filled hessian sacks piled on the racking at the rear. One by one, he lifted and carried them to the car, heaving them first onto his knee and then through the opening. That will have to do. With the temperature dropping fast, he couldn't risk the bird dying because of the cold. He took the blade from his belt and threw it into the cab. It bounced from the seat onto the floor. The sacks, he realised, had blocked his way back into the vehicle.

What was that? He cocked his ear. Rats?

The frenzied sound of timber shattering sent a chill through him. A shiny snout appeared in the rear corner, dusted by dim light. Then, the wolf thrust its head right through the flimsy wooden planks.

With brute strength born of desperation, he leaned through the window and forced the first of the three sacks over the front passenger seat into the rear. Behind, a metal rack clattered to the ground. The beast now had its head and shoulders through the wall.

Feverishly, he worked to make room. Another sack thrown into the back, he calculated there wasn't time to clear the other one. He launched headfirst into the vehicle to the accompaniment of wild scrabbling approaching as he wriggled over the logs on the front seat.

Frantic, he rolled onto his back and hauled his legs inside. Almost too late, he remembered the window. With his finger on the control button, the glass lifted halfway. Come on, come on!

Suddenly, teeth clacked against the glass, the wolf chomping on the rising edge. He prayed the mechanism would hold.

Its snout poked through the gap, filling the car with rank breath. Jericho balled his left hand into a fist with his right finger still on the button and jabbed hard, connecting with soft flesh. 'Hold on to that, you fucker!'

The window slid home.

For a moment, he sat while his heart rate subsided before reversing the vehicle to the front entrance of his home. Oh shit, the gun. No use worrying about it now.

He wound down the glass, turned off the ignition, leaned over, unlocked the door, and again, using the car as a barrier, climbed out and unloaded the sacks into the lobby. When he'd finished, he pressed the security fob and watched the window close, securing the vehicle.

Jericho hefted the first bag of logs into the lounge. 'Now we're okay,' he said, stacking more timber into the grate.

The house creaked as the last traces of warmth disappeared. His breath frosted the air with ephemeral clouds drawn inexorably towards the grate. A sound akin to the scratch of chimney brushes swept down the flue.

What the fuck? Adjusting to the gloom, he gazed into the darkness of the fireplace.

A pile of soot flumped onto the dying embers, extinguishing them. Drops of inky water fell, forming tiny craters on its blackened surface. Christ. That's never happened before. The weather cowl was missing, for sure. A vision of the wolf struck him, stalking across the roof, butting the clay pots from the brick stack before squeezing headfirst into the enlarged aperture.

Knife at the ready, Jericho sank to his knees, shuffled to the hearth and peered up into the dark recess of the chimney shaft. No way. A moment passed. Was it nothing more than soot dislodged by the wind fluting the exposed terracotta flues at the top? Despite his doubts, he dashed to the kitchen for lighter fuel.

66

Chapter 11

In the lounge, Chantelle stood close to Jack and smoothed creases from her blue uniform before folding it neatly into a bag ready for work. The switch from her prior position in the children's behavioural unit to nursing was supposed to be only temporary. One had long hours, while the other had taken a toll on her marriage. C'est la vie. Right now, there were more pressing concerns. 'I'm worried about your father.'

Jack looked up from the pile of paperwork spread over the table. 'Me too, but he'll work it out.'

'I don't know. Something bothers me about all the things that don't add up.'

'Babe, for all his drinking, he's a survivor. Come through far worse than a little storm.'

'He does not tell you everything,' she said. 'Your perception of him is outdated. He's older now.' She squeezed his hand.

'Mmm, but the thing is, he's always been insular, even before Mum died. Now, his world is smaller. Himself and a bottle of whisky. That's all he wants.'

'Jack, that is a harsh appraisal. He cares for you and Emily.'

'Well, he has a funny way of showing it. I'd never hear

from him if I didn't make the effort. He's given up on life.'

'Why then does he learn le Français?'

Jack shrugged. 'Maybe he watches European movies? I didn't ask him.'

'Does he go to class?'

'I think it's an online course.'

'You *think?*' Chantelle wagged a finger at him. 'Exactly what do you talk to your father about?'

'Okay, babe. Where are we going with this?'

'You speak with your father. I ask if he's okay. You tell me he is. I am happy. Today, I find you have concerns for him. Now, I also am concerned.'

Jack lifted her hand to his cheek. 'I'll talk to him in the morning when the telephone lines work.'

'Emily is awake now?'

He checked his watch. 'I'd hope so. It's just after 10 am. I'll catch her later when she's on a break. Weird to think it's Friday in Australia, and we still have eight hours of Thursday to go.'

'Time zones. Fascinating,' Chantelle resumed control of her hand, bunched his fingertips together and kissed them. 'What was it your father said? No matter where we are in the world, we all see the same full moon at midnight.'

'So true. I saw it last night and thought about him. Have done ever since he said that to Emily and me when we went our separate ways.'

'Tell me again, how did your parents meet?'

'You asked me this the night we met.'

'Our future depended on what you told me,' she said. 'Did you know that?'

Jack grinned. 'If only I'd known then what I know now.'

Chantelle narrowed her eyes.

'Okay, okay. Dad was a soldier—'

'C'mon! Not just any soldier.'

'No, he wasn't. He fought in trouble spots all over the world. Took part in the Iranian Embassy siege.'

Chantelle's eyes shone. 'Go on.'

'He met Mum at a place called Hadleigh Castle later that year. She was with her older sister and her son, Charlie. The boy was four, I think. They turned their backs for a moment, and the next thing, gasps from the picnicking crowds alerted them. Charlie had somehow climbed to the top of a ruin.'

'Boys, eh?'

'He got stuck at around thirty feet up. A few dads gathered at the base; everyone shouted at Charlie not to move. Luckily, he did as he was told, but these men dithered. Mum and her sister were frantic. One bloke began to climb. The crowd held their breath. He only made it halfway before giving up. He said he'd sooner not risk the boy's safety. Against what everyone was saying, Charlie stood. Shook so badly he looked about to fall. People had to hold my aunt back. Then, out of nowhere, this man arrived and went up the wall like a mountain goat. He grabbed Charlie and brought him back down. Everyone went wild with applause. That was the first time my parents met.'

Chantelle's face glowed with pride. 'The military is in

69

your blood, yet you did not serve.'

'Mum didn't want that for me.'

She nodded. 'And your father?'

Jack laughed. 'He brought me up like a soldier.'

'He was strict, non?'

'We hunted together when I was old enough. Dad taught me to build shelter, light a fire, shoot, use a knife, and much more. I never thought of him as strict.'

'So, you were close?'

'We were once…' His lips formed a grim line. 'I didn't change that. He did.'

'I'm sorry,' she said. 'I ask so many questions. A habit of my job. Your father's soldier days… did he speak of them?'

'No,' Jack said. 'I gave up asking. Mum said he never told her much, either. She knew he'd been a sniper, sometimes spent days on his own.'

'The solitude…' She nodded. 'It makes sense.'

'How?'

'His reaction to your mother's death.'

'I'm not sure I know what you mean?'

'His reluctance to talk, I feel, was a sign he'd carried out duties he wasn't proud of.'

'You can't analyse him like a child, babe.'

'True, I specialise in child psychology, but the effects of trauma and grief are similar, non?' She smiled sympathetically. 'He buried those memories and made his transition into civilian life a success. When your mom died—'

'It opened the floodgates. Explains a lot, but I still can't see him until next year.'

Chantelle picked up her coat from the stand by the door and shrugged it over her shoulders. 'Call Emily,' she said.

Jack shrugged. 'And say what?'

'Chéri, I have to run.' She blew a kiss, unlatched the door, and shouted over her shoulder, 'See you in the morning.'

'Drive carefully,' he said.

Chapter 12

Jericho sat on a footstool beside the crane, watching her. He'd uncovered her head earlier, having rationalised she'd breathe easier. She'd also stand a better chance of survival. The longer he stared, the more convinced he became she showed signs of recovery. Her beak was wider apart than it had been when he'd initially laid her down; he believed he also saw movement in her throat. Tenderly, he reached down and stroked her neck.

'A Siberian crane, no less. Considering the storm's severity, you must have blown in with the Beast from the east. I guess you left it too late to migrate for winter, then the weather caught up and swept you off course?' A rare smile lit his face. 'I appreciate you don't understand me. I speak little Russian, I'm afraid. Nyet, vodka and viski. That's about all.' When was the last time I mixed vodka and whisky? Anita's funeral. Oh, God…

His mouth dry, he licked his lips and glanced towards the kitchen, but averted his eyes before they adjusted to the gloom.

Amazed at how adrenaline negated the effects of alcohol and now in relative safety, he basked in a strange and rootless feeling as if he'd emerged from the woods but was still hopelessly lost. Come on. Take control.

He shook his head to clear it and glanced at his mobile. Still no connection.

Jericho rose from the stool, stretched out the stiffness in his lower back, and walked into the kitchen. He opened a drawer and, rummaging around, found the needed components. The ballpoint of a Bic biro pen gripped tight between thumb and forefinger; he withdrew the innards, leaving the outer tube intact. Next, he pulled up the stopper on an old cyclist's drinking bottle and taped the makeshift plastic straw into the mouthpiece with duct tape. He squeezed a puff of air into his face and, satisfied the contraption would work, stepped across to the sink to draw water into it.

Back on the stool, he shifted the crane's beak upwards and administered two drops of water through the gap onto her tongue, triggering a reflex. He smiled, a mix of joy and relief. 'Yes, Birdy,' he whispered. 'That's it, you drink.' Careful not to overdo it, he allowed her a little more before placing the bottle on the floor. 'When you recover, I'll do us something to eat. I hope you like fish fingers.' An image of the pair of them seated at the dining table made him smile. 'Just kidding. When you're better, I'll let you go.'

Jericho's thoughts returned to the wolf. A chill ran through him. His gaze drifted to the fire.

Gusts of wind siphoned the air out of the room and into the chimney. The flames flickered rhythmically, high and low, resembling tribal dancers. Visions conjured from his past arrived, accompanied by the sound of drums. He and his troop posed as mercenaries on a covert mission in Africa. At night, closing in on their target, they'd seen chanting villagers circling a bonfire, holding aloft fiery torches, feet stamping to the thudding beat. Time was of the essence. With no way round or through the valley without making contact, they'd opted for the direct approach.

The tribes-people stared warily before turning away to

focus on their own troubles.

A child cowered on all fours in the centre, illuminated by the fire. Impossible to determine if it were a boy or girl, the feral creature scrabbled around anticlockwise, in the opposite direction to the dancers, a demonic scowl upon its face. The pounding beat, movement and vocals pitched into a frenzy; the child stiffened as if electrified and then collapsed nose-first into the dirt.

Jericho felt icy cold. 'Christ,' he said. 'What's happening to me?'

Was it possible the spirit which possessed the child in Africa had hitched a ride with him, biding its time to manifest itself? He held his arms out straight ahead of him. His fingers trembled.

Jericho stood, and, approaching the window overlooking the woodshed, spoke into the darkness. 'You aren't of this world. I know that, but why did you latch onto me?'

The house lights hummed, the bulb behind him sputtering on and off before it finally lit. Pale and ghostly, an image loomed behind his reflection in the glass.

His focus shifted from outside.

Jericho turned slowly.

Birdy's pink eyes settled on his. She seemed to measure him.

Chapter 13

Jack speed-dialled Emily on the landline. Wearily, he wondered if his thoughts transmitted faster through the ether than through the wire, if that mode of communication was possible. His fingers drummed on the smoked glass table. When he finally heard the dial tone, it was faint and vaguely musical, chirruping up the line all the way from Melbourne.

'Come on,' he said, willing her to answer.

'Hello?'

'At bloody last.'

'What?' she said, indignant. 'I picked up almost right away.'

He laughed. 'The signal must have bounced off every satellite we've got up there before landing in Australia. Did you phone Dad?'

'I tried a few times. I reported a fault when I couldn't get through on his landline or mobile. There was a big snowstorm over there. Power lines down all over the place.'

'Yes, I saw that on the internet.' Jack paused. 'I think we'll need to focus more on him now.'

Emily paused. 'I agree. Neither of us talks with him enough. We've allowed him to slip further away.'

'You're right; that probably accounts for a lot.'

'Is there something else?'

'Well, Chantelle and I went online to research some things he'd mentioned. How much of what he said is real or imagined is anyone's guess, but some of it fell into place.'

'Like what?'

'You were busy when I called. I didn't tell you everything. Dad told me about a stranger who warned him about the wolf who appeared later in this dream—'

'Little brother, I think it's a mistake to indulge his imaginings, mean as that may sound.'

'I don't buy that, sis.'

'The whole thing is something he's concocted. Part of a shell he's built around himself.'

'Whatever it is, he won't accept help to deal with it. He sees that as a weakness. I'm going to ask you to do something because I can't do it myself.'

'Spit it out.'

'Can you go check on him?'

'Now?' Emily exhaled hard into the receiver. 'I'm a teacher. I couldn't make it before Christmas.'

'And I'm up for a promotion!'

'So, your job's more important than mine?'

'Sis, it's a major setback if I don't get that position.'

'Christ, listen to us! His welfare is more important than either of our jobs. One of us needs to make the trip.'

'You're right, but whoever it is, he won't appreciate us just turning up, and if we announce our intentions, he'll say no.'

'There's no easy way around it.'

'Emily, do me a favour? I'll send you a link so you can monitor when the lines in Scotland are back up and call him when they are. I'll do the same. See how he is and decide from there?'

'Yes. I'll try to persuade him to come over before Christmas. I'll tell him the warm weather will be good for him, and he can be on his own all day if that's what he chooses.'

'Let me know what he says.'

Chapter 14

Birdy followed Jericho as he wandered from room to room. Perturbed, yet strangely flattered, he wondered what the low warbling coming from her throat meant. He kept her away from the windows, figuring if she saw the wolf, she might relapse into shock, but still, there was no sign of it.

He skipped ahead. She sped up. Fast or slow, she remained in step with him. If he dipped lower to lengthen his stride, the bird did the same. 'Are you aping me?' Suddenly, he stopped and, turning to face her, stood with his arms out, cruciform.

The crane spread her wings.

Jericho shifted weight from his left to his right foot and sidestepped.

She echoed his movements.

Puzzled, he said, 'What kind of game is this?'

The crane cocked her head from side to side. 'Let's research you online.'

Jericho knew he should arrange for animal rescue to check her over, but with everything still snowbound, it could be days before they'd send anyone. Besides, she seemed fine. 'As soon as it's safe, I'll let you go, okay?' He headed for the study.

The computer fired up. An image of Anita and the kids taken the week before she died appeared on-screen. Birdy gawped at the bright monitor.

He lingered before clicking through to search Google.

Siberian crane. "Among the cranes, this bird makes one of the longest migrations. The eastern population winters on the Yangtze River and Lake Poyang in China, and the western population in Fereydoon Kenar in Iran."

'Jesus, Birdy. How on earth did you end up here?'

Oblivious to the pictures of her own kind, she tapped at the screen occasionally as Jericho delved into what zookeepers and wildlife experts had to say about cranes. Her diet included fish, cranberries and small rodents. He had blueberries, and if he cut off the batter from fish fingers, he wondered if she'd eat the meat inside.

"Whatever the species, the hatchling begins life equipped with a pre-programmed vocabulary. A highly effective set of peeping sounds for the first year, the pitch and intensity attributed to a variety of meanings, from 'Feed me,' to 'I want some attention.'"
'I wonder if there's a recording of that warbling you do?' At the first sample, Birdy's neck straightened as she zeroed in on the source of the sound. She looked increasingly confused as he listened to every recording he could find. Finally, coming up with something close, he read the caption underneath it. 'Parental attention?' he said. 'You're no hatchling, so it can't be that.' Scrolling the pages, he stopped to read further. "Imprinting. Where a newly hatched chick follows the first moving object they meet after birth. They become socially attracted."

Jericho pushed himself away from the desk, the castors on his chair rumbling across the floorboards. The bird

79

watched him rise. 'So, you banged your head. Lost your memory, and then as you regained consciousness, you reset yourself, and now think I'm your parent?' With Birdy in tow, he walked to the kitchen. 'I'm going to come back to those sound and video clips. You'll never speak human, but what if I learn Crane?' At the refrigerator, he opened the door and took out a half-empty punnet of blueberries. She watched as he offered them to her, pecking at them only after she'd observed him eat one. 'That's it, eat a few more.'

The telephone rang. Jericho glanced at the screen. The time needed resetting. 'Ems?'

'Hi, Dad. You back online then?'

'It's late, love.'

'I know. I heard about the storm. Just making sure you're okay?'

Birdy focused on the handset, tilting her head, first one way, then the other. Jericho turned his back on her.

'Are you still there?'

'Yes, I'm still here. Look, can we talk tomorrow? I was just getting ready for bed.'

The crane's beak clacked against the plastic case of the phone. 'Get off!' he whispered harshly.

'Sorry?'

'Not you, love,' he said.

'Have you got someone there with you?' Emily's voice rose high, laden with suspicion.

'No!' Jericho regretted the emphasis.

'Who is it?'

'It's no one.' Birdy lined up another strike. 'Look, I've got to go. I'll call you tomorrow.'

'You never want to talk, do you, Dad?'

His heart sank. Em, how could I possibly explain? 'Tomorrow,' he said, then disconnected the call.

Chapter 15

Once Jericho switched his mobile off, it did not surprise him when call after call came through on the landline, each disconnecting as soon as the answerphone kicked in. And every time the phone rang, his hand hovered above it, on the verge of picking up.

'What do you say? That you don't talk because you want to minimise their grief at your eventual passing by preventing them from loving you too deeply? How will you explain that to her and Jack, soldier-boy?'

The crane regarded him with apparent interest.

'Well, I'm not listening to what she has to say tonight. I've had enough drama for today.' His head cocked, first one way, then the other, mimicking the bird. 'What would you know, anyway?'

He approached the window, wiped condensation from the glass with his sleeve, leaned on the sill board and peered out. Nothing. No sight, smell, or sound. 'You're still out there, somewhere. Are you dug in waiting for me?' Could be the storm eventually drove it off, and it's now gone off to haunt someone else?

About to turn away, he stared deeper into the shadows of moonlit darkness. The outline of the woodshed became clearer. Shit, I didn't close the door. The aperture yawned black in the silvery haze.

'I know where you are,' he whispered.

As if on cue, a cloud of frosted breath appeared, and from behind it, two glints of jewel-like steely grey emerged.

Jericho bared his teeth and banged his fist on the window. 'What do you want from me?'

The wolf's eyes didn't waver from his as it shrank slowly back out of sight.

As he considered calling the police, a scenario played out in his imagination.

'A wolf, sir?'

'That's what I said.'

'No wolves are running wild in Scotland, sir,' the duty sergeant said wearily.

'I saw it, I'm telling you.' No way would he say it had also chased him. 'It tore a hole in the shed!'

'Could have been a badger. One of those could've done that, sir.'

'With a shoulder height the same as mine? I know what I saw.'

What if they came to search and found nothing but windblown, unrecognisable tracks? They'd want to question him further. Come inside the house. Discover Birdy. They'd call in Animal Rescue. His heart descended into his belly as if he'd pushed the down button in an elevator. He didn't want that. Not before he'd nursed her completely back to health. She'd given him an objective, and he needed to see it through.

Jericho stoked the grate and refilled it with logs.

'I'll sleep down here tonight. I don't know about you.'
He pulled the blanket from the floor and buried himself
underneath full length on the sofa.

The absence of whisky kept him awake longer than he
would have liked. Just outside the glowing orange halo of
the fire, he watched the crane tilt her body, balance on one
foot and, folding the other leg, draw it up into her plumage.
Her neck snaking to one side, she buried her head beneath a
wing. At some indeterminate point, he'd fallen into a deep
sleep, where unanaesthetised by alcohol for the first time in
many years; his mind plumbed the darkest depths of his
soul.

Chapter 16

The violence of the bear attack in the film gripped Jack so completely that he didn't hear the phone ring at first. He hit the pause button and dived the length of the sofa to grab it, the tips of his fingers knocking the handset from its cradle to the floor. 'Shit!'

A tinny voice said, 'Hello?'

'Wait a sec,' he shouted as he stood, reached down to pick up the receiver, and then flopped down onto the beige leather cushions.

'Are you there or not?' Emily said, her voice terse.

'I'm sorry, sis, you rang me right in the middle of The Revenant, and I dropped the phone. Did you talk to him?'

'Oh, I said plenty.'

'What did he say?'

'Not a lot. Couldn't wait to get me off the line.' Emily paused. 'I think he had a woman with him.'

Jack took a deep breath. 'It might do him good.'

'Yes, and I agree, but come on. You don't snub your daughter like that because you're... I mean, I heard her making these weird noises, and she obviously didn't give a damn that I knew she was there. She wouldn't leave him alone while he was talking to me.'

'Whoever she is...' he said. 'You aren't keen on her already.'

'He never really talks, anyway. Everything is just glossed over. I'm so pissed off with him.'

'Did you tell him that?'

'Jack, the phone was down before you could say, Neighbours!'

'But you said, you said plenty?'

'Grrrr,' Emily said. 'I thought, I'm not having this. Just couldn't help myself. I rang him back. He must have guessed I would because he'd turned his mobile off. So, then I tried the house phone. When he wouldn't answer, I left him a shitty message?'

'I wish you'd stop doing that Australian question thing at the end of your sentences. What did you say?'

'I was hopping mad—'

'Emily! What did you say in the message?'

'I told him he's selfish. He never loved us. We were better off without him! I just lost it. Could have said more. I don't remember.'

'I wish you hadn't done that. You had no business including me in your spite.'

'It just came out.'

'We...' Jack allowed the word to hang. 'Are supposed to be supporting him. I've felt like that a thousand times but never voiced it. How do you think he'll react when he plays your message back?'

'Oh, God,' she said. 'Maybe I can text him, *sorry?*'

'I hope you haven't pushed him further away. I'll call him tomorrow. Pointless trying now if he's busy. I'll tell him you called me, upset and all that.'

'Bye,' Emily whispered and cut the connection.

Jack put the phone down, shuffled along the sofa, and hit play on the remote, his thoughts no longer on Leonardo Di Caprio's battle for survival.

Chapter 17

Jericho woke clammy with sweat, his heartbeat elevated. His eyes cracked open, reluctant to break the seal between himself and the outside world. The chill in the room was oppressive and lay heavy on his damp face. Vague recollections of unquiet dreams surfaced and fell away. An underlying sense of impending doom circled him, threatening to burst forth at any second. Oh, God. Is any of this real?

Panic swelled. Tight-chested and dry-mouthed, he couldn't decide if the cause was fear, abstention or a combination of both. Whichever it was, he knew this was just the start. 'Hold it together, old son.'

A grey, pink-eyed apparition loomed above him.

'Jesus,' he mumbled. 'You frightened the life out of me.'

His hands shook as he extricated them from under the blanket. After hours without a drink, his movements didn't flow naturally. Willpower alone directed them. Cold perspiration stung his eyes, blurring his vision. He blinked rapidly to clear them, then lifted his head.

In the fireplace, seven embers winked ruby-like among the dark ashes, clinging to life. There once was a fire in you, old boy. That single thought triggered thousands. Demons arose, demanding atonement. The gates of self-control buckling, Birdy padded closer. She observed him sidelong as if wary of his mood.

Jericho threw off the blanket, swung his legs to the floor, and sat on the edge of the bed. His whole body ached. A nip of whisky. That's all I need.

In the kitchen, the red light on the answering machine flashed as he passed.

He stopped. It had to be Emily. 'I didn't mean it, girl,' he said as if she were there in the room. Nausea swept over him. Unsteady on his feet, he lurched forward and grabbed the counter with both hands.

Shaking, his finger hovered over the play button.

The crane rested her head against his arm.

'Mother always said if you've nothing good to say, say nothing. But that was mum. Not Emily.'

The delete key drew his attention like a magnet, but the pull of the bottle on the counter was stronger. In the flickering candlelight, the seductive silhouette swayed like a siren clothed in shimmering gold, singing promises of sweet solace.

Hands trembling, Jericho reached for the whisky. Feverish, he spun off the cap.

A scent of moist peat drifted into his nostrils. He leaned back on the counter, licked his lips and whispered, 'You can't keep away, can you?'

About to drink, he caught Birdy's accusatory stare. 'Don't look at me like that,' he snarled.

She dipped her head, but did not take her eyes from him.

'Oh, you're disappointed? Is that it? Well, what's it to you? You aren't family.'

89

The bottle touched his lips. He tilted his head, one eye fixed on the bird. A connection, transcending time, fluttered between them like a butterfly on a high summer breeze, transporting him to a field of blue forget-me-nots.

A red tartan blanket spread out before them; two-year-old Emily was asleep at their feet. Anita had one hand on her swollen belly; the other raked gently through the tiny blooms. 'We walked miles to get here,' she said. 'Why did you choose this field, Jerry?'

Jericho smiled and dropped back onto his elbow, regarding her thoughtfully. 'No special reason.'

Emily stirred. Anita soothed her, then gazed out over the swaying carpet of blue. 'Did you know that giving someone these flowers means you promise you'll always remember them, no matter what?'

'I didn't.' He grinned and rolled over.

Her fingers closed, and she plucked a handful of stems, arranging them into a small bouquet. 'Here you are,' she said, holding them out to him.

Jericho smiled and offered her the bunch he'd picked when she'd fussed over Emily. 'Snap,' they said in unison and melted into each other's arms.

Afterwards, Anita said, 'Can I ask you something?'

Her tone aroused suspicion. Jericho hesitated, knowing what the next question would be. 'About my nightmares?'

'Yes.' Her fingers folded over his.

'I don't even know myself.'

'You must remember *something?*'

'Nope,' he said, shaking his head. 'Not a thing.'

'You must know why you wake up screaming?'

For a moment, he descended into darkness. For a moment, he almost saw, but something inside him shut it down. 'Neet, can we change the subject?'

'Jerry, *please* talk to someone.'

'Whatever it is, I will get through it, but I must do it alone.'

Anita seemed to sense the finality of his words. She cleared her throat. 'Jerry, I'm scared for you. Where will it lead if you just keep drinking more and more?'

'I told you, love. I'll sort it.'

Christ, I never did. The taste of regret, a bitter tang; he lowered the bottle and tilted it as if to pour it down the plughole, then changed his mind. He replaced the cap and tucked the whisky away in a cupboard. Birdy seemed to nod approval.

Jericho wandered to the kitchen window and looked out. With the bird now ever-present by his side, he watched thin clouds sail across the moon in the predawn sky.

Although he couldn't see it, he sensed the wolf was still out there.

Chapter 18

Chantelle stopped by the hospital exit to let an ambulance driver stomp through the revolving doors, brushing snow from his face and hair and patting down his clothes. 'Eight degrees,' he announced, 'and more pig weather on the way.'

'That is what I heard too,' she said and grimaced. 'I'd best get going.'

'You live far?'

'Forest Lawn Heights,' she said.

'There's an accident on Memorial. Traffic's backed up. It's gonna take you a while to get home.'

'Just my luck.' Chantelle zipped the front of her coat, took a deep breath and walked out into the blizzard. She scrunched her face against the cold and crossed the road, hurrying to the near-empty car park. Streetlamps lent a bizarre effect to the swirling flakes, transforming them into swarms of white moths caught in fields of brilliance. She rushed to her vehicle and opened the door.

A pile of snow fell onto her seat. 'Merde!' After sweeping it off, she recovered the scraper from the floor and cleared the windows before setting off for home.

She joined the tailback of traffic at 7:31 am. Still dark, the glare of oncoming headlights beamed into her tired eyes. Resigned to the delay, her fingers rebelled by drumming on the steering wheel. She sighed. At least there's no more work until Tuesday. Her last twelve-hour shift had run to fifteen. A colleague had an appointment, and Chantelle agreed to arrive three hours early to cover for her. How much time had she given up free of pay? She dismissed the thought without attempting a calculation. It was an occupational hazard. Sometimes, she and Jack were like two ships passing in the night. She'd arrive home, shower, and then sleep while Jack fixed breakfast. He worked from home most days, and her shift rotas meant more time together.

A gap opened in the line of cars next to her. She indicated and edged into it.

Her thoughts drifted to Jericho. I wonder what is happening to him? He has too many secrets. It does him no good. Can he not see he ruins his own life? At least Jack doesn't drink.

His father's secrecy left him mostly unaffected, yet he still had issues. Her time working in the children's behavioural health department taught her that. The refusal to admit any dysfunction in the home was one of them, his rigid self-sufficiency another, but those things helped mould the man she loved.

The gain from switching lanes slowly reversed, and she found herself trailing six cars behind her original position. C'est la vie.

The National came on the radio. She turned the music up. Slender fingers tapping the steering wheel, she lowered her chin and sang along in a pseudo baritone, hopelessly attempting to match the depth of the lead singer's voice.

"Today,

You were far away,

93

And I,

Didn't ask you why...."

The song reminded her of Jack. Sometimes, she missed working with disturbed children, but it placed a strain on their relationship. Jack bottled it up rather than talked. Little by little, she'd chipped away at his defences. Whilst he was unhappy about the stresses she'd taken on, he recognised the worthiness of the role and said nothing. That's why she returned to general nursing.

She switched the music off.

After an endless hour on the road, Chantelle turned into her street. Moments later, the car crunched through the six inches of fresh snow on their driveway.

Quietly letting herself in, she slipped off her coat and shoes. She cocked her head, listening. Not a sound.

A shaft of light spilt onto the floor from an open door down the hallway, disappearing the instant she switched on the lamp in the hall. Something's wrong. He never leaves the light on when he goes to bed. Has he been drinking? I bet he's left a mess for me in there.

Torn between tiredness and needing to tidy, Chantelle crept barefoot into the room.

He'd left magazines scattered all over the coffee table and thrown everything around in a semblance of how she liked things. She plumped the cushions and rearranged them. A remote control poked out from beneath the sofa, along with an empty DVD box. Chantelle eased it out and examined the cover.

The Revenant. 'You could not wait, could you?' she whispered.

94

They'd talked about watching it ever since seeing the trailer at the movies. Friends who'd seen it warned her of the violence of the bear attack. 'It's like a rape,' they'd said. It didn't put her off. She loved Leonardo Di Caprio. Buying the movie to enjoy at home made sense. Now Jack would have to sit through it again at the weekend.

At the end of the sofa, tucked between the arm and the wall, she discovered an empty glass and, stooping to collect it, sniffed the residue. She smiled. Blackcurrant. Once she'd put it in the kitchen, Chantelle glanced in on him. His body formed a double hillock under the rumpled bedclothes.

She tiptoed into the bathroom, turned on the shower, and stepped into the steaming cascade.

An unholy sound came over the hiss of the powerful jets. What the hell was that? It seemed to come from the bedroom.

She shut the valve, cutting the water. Loathe to wake him, she resisted the urge to call out. Alert, she let herself out of the cubicle, grabbed a towel and rubbed herself dry, starting with her hair.

A low moan reached her. What are you dreaming about, chéri? Perhaps he heard me in the shower, and he's acting out something in his subconscious? Chantelle smiled, opened the door, and crept into the bedroom.

Jack had turned from his side. Now lying on his back with his arms outside the duvet, she saw his fingers twitch in the dim light. His eyes rolled behind his eyelids, moving lips remaining sealed as if stitched together. The sound he made sent a chill through her.

She frowned. Never before had she seen him so utterly immersed in a dream. She watched from the edge of the bed,

95

fascinated.

Almost imperceptibly, Jack's head moved from side to side. The line between his eyebrows deepened, his breathing short, becoming quicker, laboured. His jaw dropped. A sound, low, guttural, zombie-like, issued from his throat. Beneath the covers, his legs jerked, and his fingers and thumbs sprang into life like a manic puppeteer. His eyes flew open, panic-stricken.

Chantelle grabbed his shoulders and shook him. 'Jack. Chéri! Wake up.'

'Noooo!' he cried and sat up, eyes wide open, haunted and unaware of her presence.

'Are you okay?'

He slumped into her. She cradled him in her arms.

'Babe,' he gasped, 'thank God!'

'You had a nightmare, non?'

Jack struggled to control his breathing. 'My heart, Jesus, I thought it would explode.'

Chantelle's hand slid onto his chest, her eyes wide. 'Mon Dieu! It beats so fast! What were you dreaming about?'

'Something chasing me in the snow. It grabbed me from behind and threw me down. I couldn't move, couldn't fight—'

'You watched that movie, didn't you, with the bear?'

He lifted his face. Their gaze met.

'This wasn't a bear,' he whispered, wide-eyed. 'It was a wolf.'

Chapter 19

Jack shivered in Chantelle's arms. 'Baby, It seemed so real….'

She brushed a lock of damp hair from his forehead. 'I know,' she whispered.

'I'm not sure you do. I—'

'You think I never had a nightmare?'

'Not like this, you haven't.'

'Maybe not, but I watched over you.' How could she tell him she'd observed him out of curiosity?

'You could've woken me!'

Neither could she tell him she'd seen his legs cycling under the covers as if he were running from something? 'In the end, I did—'

'Jesus, babe, I could have died before that.'

'I wasn't sure it was safe. I know from studies it is best to wake from the light sleep.'

Jack's voice rose. 'Are you kidding me?'

'I am not. What I saw reminded me of children with sleep paralysis. They must learn to deal with it themselves.'

'I'm not a child.'

'Adults also suffer from it.'

Jack tilted his face so that their eyes met. 'It wasn't that, I'm telling you.'

'So, what are you saying? A demon which haunts your father has crossed the ocean to attack you, too?' Despite her mockery, the hairs on her arms prickled.

'I still can't get over you not waking me right away.'

'Did you speak with Emily?'

'That's it, change the subject.'

Chantelle pulled free. 'You have a lot on your mind. The worry for your father, the movie. It twisted into something else, et voilà, you have a bad dream. What did Emily say?'

'We had a bit of a tiff, nothing serious. Just talking about Dad sometimes does that. Then she told me she heard a woman in the background.'

'But this is good, non?'

'Baby, I've not known him to... he's never even mentioned women since Mum died.'

'He does not want to upset you.'

'No, it isn't that. Dad's not sensitive enough to consider our feelings. This is all part of whatever's happening to him.'

Chantelle yawned. 'Your father, he is having the midlife crisis.'

'Get some sleep, babe.' Jack flopped onto the bed. 'We'll talk later.'

Jericho roasted on a spit of his own making. It cranked around from his children and the opportunities to bond with them he'd pushed away, to the wolf, the crane's well-being, to the craving for drink growing stronger every hour. His mind would not quieten. It was as if he were a psychic at a busy airport, unable to tune out the myriad thoughts of others, unable to distinguish them from his own. Previously, he'd found punishing exercise a release in times of personal crisis. This time, it had taken him to the brink, releasing something he couldn't now control. Birdy observed him, bemused. 'I'm not crazy, you know,' he said. Or maybe I am? 'Come on, let's see what's going on outside.'

Together, he and the bird looked out from the windows of every downstairs room.

The storm had passed. Blackbirds and pigeons foraged in the snow. The wolf had gone; he was sure of it. Fillan had warned it would come on the Day of the Dead but never said it would stay.

He could not stomach food, so he drank tap water, ensuring Birdy ate some muesli. She messed on the floor again. Blueberries and cream. On his knees, wiping away the gloop, he retched. 'Jesus, Birdy.'

Earlier, she had followed him upstairs, dogging his every move while he gathered fresh clothes. Jericho locked her out of the bathroom while he showered, ignoring her plaintive calling. A man needs his privacy. Once finished, he opened the door. She purred.

Amid an overwhelming torrent of thoughts, he forced himself to continue researching crane behaviour and human interaction. After restarting the page several times, he realised he wasn't absorbing any of it. I need to get this on paper.

He rummaged through the cupboard under the stairs, pulling out a dusty old ledger. A cloud of dust wafted into Birdy's enquiring face when he blew it clean. 'Sorry about that,' he said. She blinked in disapproval.

Next, he opened the kitchen drawer, took out a pen, and sat down to write. The biro proved an irritation to her, and she attacked it repeatedly.

'Do that again,' Jericho groaned. 'And it's off to another room for you.'

Twice more, he shoved her away. Undeterred, she persisted. The chair scraped the floor as he got to his feet. 'That's it,' he said. 'Out you go.'

She followed him into the lounge. Two steps in, he spun on his heel and exited the room before she could react, closing the door behind him.

He ambled back to the kitchen table, sat, turned the page, and wrote Friday, November 3rd, 2017.

A tapping at the hatch began, accompanied by a soft warbling. Jericho stopped writing and glanced over his shoulder. Through the glass, he saw her doleful expression. 'For Christ's sake. Don't look at me like that!'

He continued with his journal for a few minutes before succumbing to her calls for unison. 'Birds will be birds, eh?' He stroked her head as she high-stepped out. Passing through the kitchen, he grabbed another pen from the drawer. 'Let's try you with this.'

Once again seated at the table, he dropped the spare ballpoint on the floor. The crane picked it up with ease. Jericho tuned out the sound of Birdy's new toy clattering each time she dropped it and her beak scratching to retrieve it. He resumed writing, his focus transcending everything around him. Part of him long detached, reunited. Clouds parted. He knew what he had to do. Turning a new page, he jotted three headings which covered his life as he saw it.

Childhood and growing up.

Army days.

Family.

It was the only way his children would get to know the man their father had been. After some thought, he added a fourth line.

Winter.

Chapter 20

Jericho stood at the window, hollow-eyed, contemplating what he'd written so far. He faced his reflection in the dark glass, a parody of the man he used to be. Every year, life grows colder. Is this the winter of my life? Made colder because I hid myself away?

The journal, sketched out in a shaky hand, covered many boyhood adventures. He'd lost touch with his friends when he left school, their faces as fresh as the last time he'd seen them, unwearied by age.

Satisfied he'd covered all events that might interest his children, he moved on to his army days and the many battles he'd survived. That jigsaw took time to fit together, and he was fast running out of pieces. No doubt he'd lived on autopilot for a whole chunk of it. Lucky to come through unscathed. He'd always been lucky. Between missions, he'd met Anita, but between which ones? He couldn't think. If you'd asked him if he believed in love at first sight, he'd have said emphatically no. Looking back on his first meeting with her, that's precisely what it was.

For the first time, he'd been reluctant to return to the welcoming arms of the military.

Snatches of memory twirled like black feathers caught in a vortex. A familiar drumbeat directed the cadence of his heart to meet its pounding rhythm. Swept up in those fleeting moments, he landed at the head of a valley, the village they'd passed through below, bonfires still blazing, each soldier carrying the aftermath of the exorcism they'd witnessed in their own way, in his case, behind a mask of inscrutable professionalism. Jericho's patrol, their faces darkened and streaked with camouflage paint, appeared primal and at odds with the combat fatigues, helmets and night vision goggles they wore. A mist crept down the hillside and merged with the impenetrable curtain his mind had created.

He blinked, surprised he still gazed into the night. His focus adjusted. Reflected in the window, Birdy by his side, he threw an arm around her. The two of them appeared monochrome in the dim light, captured at that moment like an early photographer's portrait. A smile tinged with sadness crept over his face. 'Look at us,' he said. 'How will I ever let you go?'

She cocked her head and then shuffled close as the moon disappeared behind a dark cloud.

He turned away from the window, wondering what further long-buried demons his increasing sobriety would unleash. At the opposite end of the kitchen, the blinking red light of the answering machine nagged at him. He returned to the table and wrote, *Family.*

Pen poised above the page, his attention again wandered. He couldn't relax. The emotional undercurrent building in him would sweep him away if he did. He'd let his guard down, first with Emily, now with Jack. A moment of reverie caught hold. Jack was a small boy mowing the grass next to him with a toy Flymo, aping his every move, stopping to follow him to the compost heap to empty his little machine

103

on the fresh cuttings Jericho deposited there.

So tightly bound by the emotional detachment required for his role in the army, he'd failed his family while in service and continued to fail them. It didn't matter how he framed it. To claim he'd been that way to make it easier on them if the worst happened to him would never wash with them.

He missed the childhoods he'd missed out on, this disconnection he'd carried on for too long.

Jericho put his face in his hands, the biro hard and cool, dug in from temple to jawline. He felt the plastic bow. His eyes stung. A wave of nausea came over him. His stomach cramped, and bile rose in the back of his throat.

Make it stop.

For a moment, everything ceased.

When he was a child, he'd visited the Sistine Chapel with his parents. Botticelli's Temptations of Christ flashed before him. Jesus with the devil. An arm sweeping the landscape, the fallen angel promising him the world. He'd made no sense of it at all back then. An unfathomable feeling of despair latched onto him, and with it, the need to escape, which now seemed more important than his desire to remember.

The phantom of a familiar scent teased his taste buds. Darkness clouding his judgement, he salivated and licked his lips. Just one won't hurt.

The pen snapped between his fingers, surprising him.

When he looked up from the table, the expression of bewilderment on Birdy's face, if that's what it was, grounded him in an instant.

He slid from the chair onto his knees and walked his hands forward into a press-up position. His arms protested, not yet recovered from earlier. Palms beneath his shoulders, the small of his back straight, he unlocked his elbows and trembled as he lowered himself. He pushed up. One.

On the next repeat, the crick in his neck joined the protest. Two. When did I allow myself to get so weak?

He concentrated on completing another rep, forcing his arms to straighten. Three. Birdy stepped closer, her feet within inches of his face. He held the position, fascinated by the texture of her pink legs and feet. Three claws with a stubbed one on the back he'd not noticed before. They looked soft. 'Do not distract me,' he gasped, imagining her head cocked as she observed from above.

He pressed on, punishing himself, no longer afraid that his subconscious would give up more from its depths.

Chapter 21

Jack scowled at the calculation displayed on his computer. It couldn't be right; it had to be an input error. He sighed and scrolled through the figures, looking for an obvious mistake. 'Gotcha! How the hell did I miss that decimal point?' He made the correction, and with the total now in line with expectations, he concluded the substructure quantities and saved the file. His mobile lit and vibrated, spinning a half-circle on the smoked glass top before he snatched it up. 'Babe?'

Chantelle's giggle came from the bedroom, as well as through the phone. She disconnected.

He checked his watch. 12:55 pm. That girl gets by on no sleep at all. Rising from the chair, he strode from the lounge to join her.

An hour later, he lay propped on pillows, his chin resting on Chantelle's head. 'If I were a smoker, I could use a cigarette right now.'

'Me too!' She laughed, her warm breath rippling the hairs on his chest. 'You know, I have been thinking, chéri.' Her fingers light on his belly, she traced the trail of hair to his groin.

His voice groggy, he mumbled, 'That tickles.'

'You like this better?' she said and pinched him.

'Ouch. What's that for?'

'You are not listening.' She laughed. 'I am not back to work until Tuesday. You can take Monday off?'

'You want to go somewhere?' he said.

'Let's visit your father.'

Jack rolled from beneath her. 'You can't be serious?'

'Why not?'

He sat up, his fingers steepled on either side of his nose. 'It's a fifteen-hour flight. Then, the journey from the airport. By the time we got there, it would be time to come back again. And then there's the money—'

'He is your father. He is worth it, non?'

'Of course, but—'

'We could travel tomorrow. Spend all day on Sunday with him. Leave in the evening.'

'Baby, I couldn't spring that on him.'

'Then call him.'

Jack blew out his cheeks before exhaling. 'Have you checked for flights?'

'I will look while you speak with him.'

'This is madness…'

'Call your father,' she said.

Jericho stared at the pages of scribbled notes he'd

completed throughout the day. The stranger, the wolf, the crane. Anita. His children. The opportunity to forge stronger bonds with them was foregone. The army. Africa. No longer sure he'd served his full term. Why can't I remember Africa?

One subject he hadn't written about was his drinking. Every bone in his body ached. Tonight, it was worse. He blamed his exercise regime, but his addiction contrived to steer every thought, conscious or otherwise, leading him countless times to that cupboard door. To look at the bottle where a liquid genie promised three wishes. One would do. Beyond oblivion, what else was there? Finding himself there once again, he closed the door and turned towards the answering machine. The red light blinked Morse code. *Listen to me.*

Birdy nudged him with her head. He shrugged. 'What do you want?'

She raised her wings.

Jericho mocked her by standing on one leg, flapping his arms.

She echoed his moves.

He laughed and, spinning around full circle, noticed how she dipped, gaze fixed upon him, and began a dance-like routine.

Drunk with craziness, he went along with it. Hopping from foot to foot, arms out, fingers fluttering. 'What the fuck is this? You wanna dance?'

She turned her back, and tail feathers held high, presented her bottom, soliciting like a cat on heat.

'Oh, God. Birdy. No!'

The telephone rang.

He glanced at the clock. 10 pm. It can't be Emily.

'Hello?'

'How are you?' Jack said.

Do I tell him I'm not drinking? Unbidden, tears pooled in his eyes. 'Hello, boy. I'm fine.'

'That's good. Emily tried to reach you—'

'I know,' Jericho said, his voice hoarse. 'That girl is so petulant.'

'You listened to her message?'

'Not yet.'

'Have you met someone?'

'Why are you asking me that, boy?'

'It's just Emily said she thought, er, you might have had a woman with you, and that's why you didn't want to talk. She freaked a bit.'

'Is that right?' Jericho wiped his tears away and glanced at Birdy.

'She worries about you. We both do.'

'No need. I can look after myself.'

'I just phoned to say, don't listen to her message.'

Moments passed, and then Jericho said, 'Everything we do has consequences, and we must live with our choices.'

'Dad—'

'Forget it.'

109

The bird clacked her beak against the phone.

'What was that?' Jack said.

Jericho's laughter seemed inappropriate, bordering on hysteria.

'What's so funny?' Jack hadn't heard him laugh like that in years.

The laughter rumbled on.

'Dad?'

'That was hilarious.'

'Evidently,' Jack said drily.

'You wouldn't believe me if I told you.'

'Let's hear it.'

Jericho elaborated on his account of everything, deliberately excluding any mention of the wolf.

Jack chuckled. 'Chantelle will have a field day when I tell her.'

'Why?'

'A crane turns up on the anniversary of Mum's death?'

Jericho paused. 'I never gave that a thought,' he said. 'I suppose it is strange. She has that same innocence Mum never lost.'

'Well, it isn't Mum.'

'I'm just saying, that's all.'

Jack sighed. 'Are you going to let her go?'

'I'm not sure she's recovered fully. Besides, right now,

110

she's company.'

'You can't keep her. That would be wrong.'

Jericho let out a long breath. 'I know.'

'The wolf you saw in that nightmare with Mum…' Jack paused. 'What colour was it?'

'We don't talk about that anymore.'

'What colour was it?'

'Why do you ask?'

'What colour, Dad?' Jack's tone was insistent.

'Black.'

Silence gaped between them.

'Why would you ask me that?' Jericho said. 'Have you seen it too?'

'No. I was curious, that's all.' What good would it do to tell him the truth? 'We've gone off track. I rang to let you know that Chantelle and I would like to visit this weekend.'

'Boy, unless you have a helicopter, forget about it. We're completely snowbound.'

'We?'

'The bird and me.'

'Okay, Dad. I told Chantelle it was a stupid idea. I'll call again soon. Nice talking to you.'

'Hey, son, I've….'

'Yes?'

'It doesn't matter. Yes, catch up soon.'

111

The connection cut. Jericho replaced the phone. Despite his efforts to push them away, Jack had been prepared to travel four thousand miles on a whim to see him, and Emily cared enough to leave a message the boy didn't want him to hear. A lump formed in his throat. The red light goaded him. His finger hovered over the play button. Then he pressed delete.

After what Jack just said, I'll feel better with a gun in my hands, even if the creature is supernatural. He walked to the lobby, flipped on the outside light, and opened the front door.

Birdy... I can't leave her inside. If anything happens to me, she'll be trapped. What if I leave the door open and I'm wrong about the wolf?

Warm air rushed from the house and mingled with the crisp air from outside, creating a vortex that lowered the temperature exponentially. For a moment, he stood and listened. At night, there was no birdsong, nature's barometer for safety. Memories of walking through the woods with Anita and the children floated back to him. Blackbirds fled before them and perched in low branches, chittered alarm. All other species within earshot fell silent.

'When birds sing,' he said. 'We're safe. That call we just heard is for predators on the ground. The one for hawks is different.'

'I never knew that,' Anita replied.

Jericho's recollections grew. 'Yes, it's pretty much true. Once they've figured out we're no threat, they'll start calling to each other again.'

'Do they all speak the same language?' Emily asked.

Anita laughed. 'Only they know the answer to that.'

'And God,' Jack chimed. 'My teacher told us He knows everything.'

The memory faded as an owl hooted mournfully, drawing his attention. Suddenly, it swept from the woodshed to the ground, where it snatched up a small rodent and took off again. A thick clump of snow from the adjacent shrubbery flumped down as if to mark its passing.

If the wolf is still around, he isn't close. Jericho waded around the car and probed the thigh-high drifts using his foot, hoping he hadn't run over the weapon.

His legs ached from scything through the white crust. Finally, his toe connected with a solid object. He stooped to excavate the shotgun. The cold barrel sparked a chain reaction which ran into his fingers and spread through his being. Back indoors, teeth chattering, he stomped his boots clean of snow. 'Shit, I'll have to change out of these trousers.' To avoid treading wet throughout the house, he stripped them off where he stood. His mood, swinging between extremes all day, now turned to hatred. Now, there's something worthy of focus. He thought about the wolf as he dried and cleaned his weapon.

'I will find you,' he whispered.

Chapter 22

Kurt looked like a man walking a girlfriend's chihuahua while trailing Emily around the supermarket.

'Why are you hanging back?' Emily said. 'Scared your friends from the bar will see you shopping?'

'No bloody chance of that,' he said, nervously scouting the aisle. 'You wouldn't catch 'em dead in here.'

She laughed. 'You guys… What shall we get for supper?'

He grinned. 'Some tinnies? I could use a beer.'

She brandished her fist at him. 'Remind me to buy a rolling pin.'

'Speaking of which, you made it up with the old man yet?'

Emily stopped. The cart askew in the aisle. 'He knows where I am.'

'You've been hanging around with me for too long.'

'What do you mean?'

'That's what *I* would've bloody said, but it isn't you, Ems. Why don't you give it another go?'

'You could be right, Kurt. Maybe I pick up traits from the men in my life.'

'Nah, you've always been stubborn.'

She grabbed a box of pasta and pushed off with the trolley. They passed a young man stacking shelves. 'Can you point me toward the rolling pins?' Emily said.

Kurt drove while Emily sat in silence, the wind tugging at her hair as she gazed through the open window.

'You all right?' He squeezed her knee.

'Just thinking,' she said.

'About Dad?'

Emily sighed. 'I feel awful about leaving him that message.'

'You gotta talk to him.'

'That's what I tried to do, but he never answered the phone.' She shook her head. 'I wish I hadn't said those things.'

'From what I know of your old man, he's already forgotten about it.'

She turned to face him. 'Because he drinks too much?'

'No. Because your father's an emotional cripple.'

'I can say that, but I don't like it if anyone else does.'

'Ems, you can't deny he keeps his emotions guarded.'

'Of course not,' she said.

Kurt slowed down and made a right turn. 'Does he ever blow his stack?'

Emily paused. 'Not that I've ever known. If he was

angry, he'd slope off somewhere and get hammered. Mum always complained he never talked.'

'You women always say that,' he said. 'I'll bet he went off on a big bender once he heard your message.'

'He might not have heard it yet.' Emily took her phone from her pocket.

He glanced at her. 'What're you doing?'

'Sending my dad a text.'

'Just call him.'

She looked at her watch. 'It's the middle of the night in Scotland. He'll be in bed. Besides, I sent it already.'

At some indeterminable point, Jericho had fallen into a deep sleep.

A blood moon hung above the sinuous black river, illuminating a shimmering path across its waters as they made their way upcountry beneath a night sky more studded with stars than any he had seen before. The riverboat's engines were a low drone against a backdrop of raucous whoops and cries of jungle creatures. Crocodiles slid silently from the riverbank into the water, attracted by the chugging vessel, their eyes luminescent in the semi-darkness. He stood on deck and watched them approach, only to fall behind, adrift, uncannily similar to drifting logs, their scaly skin glistening bark-like in the moonlight. Aboard, apart from him, fifteen grim-faced soldiers, equally spaced on each side of the boat, sat in silence. Jericho ticked off their names in a silent roll call. Blake, Hopkins, Jones, Smith— Something buzzed, jolting him awake.

The thread of the dream vanished, sucked from his mind

like smoke up a chimney.

'What the fuck?' It took a few seconds to realise he was on the sofa. He sat up and yanked the phone from his pocket. 4:08 am.

Emily. *Sorry about the message I left on your voicemail.*

As much as it irritated him to be woken after sleeping, he guessed, for only an hour, he was pleased to hear from her. He tapped four words in reply, shivered, and rose to put more logs on the dying embers.

Afterwards, he slumped back onto the couch. Wood hissed as moisture boiled and steam evaporated through fissures in the bark. The timber crackled and spat as flames licked the newly dried surfaces, scorching them. Jericho gazed at the shadow play on the ceiling. To grow strong again, he needed sleep. He closed his eyes. What was it about Africa? It seemed like he was chasing the tail of a snake, never quite seeing its head.

He toyed with the idea of another workout. I might just collapse with exhaustion and fall back to sleep. Or my journal?

He knew he couldn't force it either way. For more exercise, he needed rest. To write more, he had to remember.

When a man buries part of himself for so long, who knows what will come out of the depths and what of it will be true?

These days, he'd have taken part in therapy. Back then, he'd simply denied he had a problem. You just grinned and bore it.

At first, he kept the drinking from his family. During the

117

day, he stayed sober but disappeared into a black hole at night.

Once Anita had gone, and the kids made lives for themselves elsewhere, his self-discipline fell away.

Not that he didn't love his children. He'd simply lost his iron will. The application of willpower was like riding a bicycle. You never forgot, but you had to be ready.

He cracked a smile. Two nights in, and I can see the light. Wait till I tell the kids. Tell them face to face. But I can't let them know yet. How can I reveal the full circumstances that led me to this? Or that fear, hatred and compassion for a bird had finally set him free?

For all his newfound strength, he still couldn't sleep.

Chapter 23

Kurt grabbed a beer from the fridge as Emily's mobile pinged a message. 'Who is it, Em?'

'My dad.'

'What'd he say?'

'Thanks for waking me.' She threw the phone onto the sofa. 'I can't do right for doing wrong.'

'Not being funny, but you bloody knew he'd be in bed.'

'I thought his phone would be off.'

Her phone rang. She stared wide-eyed at Kurt.

'Well, you gonna get it, or what?'

Emily scrambled around the island unit, which separated the lounge from the kitchen, and grabbed the phone.

'I'm so sorry, Dad. I didn't mean to wake you.'

Kurt cracked the beer open and wandered over to join her on the sofa, listening to the one-sided conversation.

'No, no, everything's fine and you?... Why aren't you sleeping?' Her brow furrowed. 'You don't sound good. I'm sorry about the message I left.' She glanced at Kurt and smiled. 'You didn't listen?... Sorry, I missed that. I'm worried about you. Do me a favour. I know you won't like it, but can we switch to FaceTime? I need to see you... I know that, but just this once. Please?'

Kurt arched an eyebrow. 'Good luck with that,' he muttered.

'It couldn't be simpler. I'll call you back. It'll say Emily wants FaceTime, and you just answer.'

'Dad?' She shrugged, bemused. 'He's gone.'

Kurt slid over and cuddled her. 'Doesn't he realise how much he hurts you? Gimme that, I'm gonna bloody phone him.'

Her mobile rang.

'Dad wants FaceTime. Can you believe it?' She bounced on the sofa and, pressing accept, held out the screen. Jericho's face was too close to the camera, looking bewildered.

'Hey, Dad!'

'Ems?'

She waved. 'I'm here.'

Kurt leaned in, 'Hi, Jerry!'

'Hi, Kurt.' Jericho half-smiled, bemused. 'I can see myself. I don't look so good.'

Emily noted the dark semicircles under her father's eyes. 'It's the middle of the night. What do you expect?'

Jericho blinked at the screen.

'Come on, say something!' she said. 'You broke up earlier. I wondered why you didn't listen to my message?'

'Sorry, this FaceTime is just too weird. Did you ask me?'

'Yes,' she said.

'I spoke to your brother. He said not to listen, so I didn't.'

'Have you met someone, Dad?' Her lower teeth scraped her top lip. 'I mean, I'm thrilled if you have.'

'I explained all this to Jack.' Jericho's eyes drifted left.

'Is she there with you now?' Emily touched her face, checking her makeup.

A flash of white came into view, and something clacked against the screen.

Emily jumped. 'What the hell was that?'

'I'm not going over it all again,' Jericho said wearily. 'You'll have to ask Jack.'

'Was that a bird?'

Jericho turned the phone toward the crane. 'Meet Birdy.'

Kurt leaned out of sight and rotated his finger beside his temple. Emily thumped his knee.

'Well, what's this all about? You can't just *not* tell me!'

Jericho rubbed an eye. 'She flew into the house the other night.'

'Through the window?'

'No,' he said, exasperated. 'Crashed into it. I thought she was dead, but I brought her inside, and now she's recovered. I'm getting tired, Ems, sorry.'

'Hey, don't go yet. I want to talk some more.'

'I have to go, but we'll chat again soon.' Jericho's finger

touched the screen. 'Don't look at me like that.'

'I didn't think you liked birds,' she said. Kurt tittered in the background.

Jericho widened his eyes. 'What makes you say that?'

'I remember when I was a little girl. You kicked a big white bird like the one you've got there.'

'No, Ems, that was a goose. This one's much bigger. Jesus, I'd forgotten all about that.' His face came alive at the memory. 'You were around five years old, and we went to a pub because there was a pond, and I knew you'd love it. You were chasing ducks.'

'Why didn't they like me?'

His voice softened. 'Of course, they liked you. They were simply scared. You got too close to a goose. Must have had eggs or something because it charged out of the bushes and went for you.'

'I was so scared.'

'And I kicked it away. Got into a terrible row with an older woman and her husband. They objected to me using violence against the bird to protect you. It wasn't that I didn't like the goose. The same way it defended its eggs, I looked out for you.'

'Remember when we were out on my first big bike, and I fell off?'

Jericho laughed. 'Yes. Scraped all your knees and refused to get back on.'

'You rode off and left me!'

'No, Ems. You left yourself. All you had to do was jump on and ride.'

122

'I never forgave you for that.'

'You didn't? Don't you remember, I waited around the corner for you? I would never have left you. I wanted you to tough it out. Learn to take the knocks and push on through.'

Emily turned away from the camera and brushed a tear from her face.

Birdy attacked the screen.

Jericho's eyes sparkled, dewy. He wiped them with his sleeve. 'I've got to go, Ems.' His voice cracked. 'We'll do this again. Soon.'

And then he was gone.

Chapter 24

Day Three. November 4th, 2017.

Muscles clenched and sweat dripping from his face, Jericho finished the last set of sit-ups. He flopped down and contemplated standing. More self-inflicted pain was needed today if he were to remain focused. When he ached, alcohol withdrawal symptoms couldn't be blamed.

He rolled onto his belly, pushed up to his knees and stood, thankful he'd completed the rest of the circuit training already.

Curious, Birdy watched him throughout. Her movements, neck dipping, hopping from foot to foot, wings rising and falling, echoed her interpretation of his moves. That she helped motivate him, he couldn't deny. At first, his interest focused on understanding her better. Now, it appeared she sought the same with him. Sometimes, they'd exchange a moment, and it seemed she'd shared some of her species' ancient wisdom with him.

Would he have begun to turn his life around and make peace with Emily if Birdy hadn't appeared when she did?

He jerked his head for the crane to follow. 'Come on, let's get you fed.'

While he drank a pint of water, the bird pecked at the muesli in the bowl he'd set down for her. 'This stuff doesn't taste of anything,' he said, scowling at the empty glass. He looked out the window. Wood pigeons filled the skeletal branches, more than he'd ever seen. All of them faced in the same direction. East.

'We'll go outside in a while. The fresh air will do both of us good.' For an instant, he thought about tethering her. 'You won't fly away, will you?' His heart confirmed the answer.

Once he'd put on his coat, Jericho picked up his shotgun and ventured outside. Sunshine lent an illusion of warmth to the crisp air. Following the crane, he closed the door and heaved his legs through the polar-like tundra.

In the trees, the pigeons shuffled nervously. They've seen my gun.

Birdy high-stepped through the snow, heading toward the rushes surrounding the pond. Her gait, seemingly hesitant, she walked onto the snow-encrusted ice.

He considered her behaviour. Had instinct guided her to the water as a potential food source? Could it be that the knock on her head hadn't entirely wiped out her memory? Would she suddenly up and leave? His heart, so sure of her earlier, plummeted at the thought. If she's meant to go, she will go.

Jericho looked up at the roosting birds. Tinged in the golden glow of sunshine, he saw everything in a new light. The symmetry of the trees struck him: the growing up, the branching out, the building of girth in the trunk sufficient to bear all the uppermost parts, which stretched like bony fingers aching to touch the heavens.

Isn't that what we all do?

Pigeons mumbled and cooed like old women gossiping. Mountains of leaden cumulonimbus gathered, and as the sun vanished behind them, the landscape fell grey. The wind rose from the east. Jericho lifted his collar against the cold and squinted. On the horizon, a shaft of light beamed through a gap in the clouds, slicing a path through the gloom, and out of it, long pewter-coloured hair flying in the breeze, a familiar stranger marched towards him with his sporran keeping time.

Jericho had no fear. He watched with a sense of detachment as Fillan arrived before him. Neither man said a word.

The highlander, in the flesh, stood taller than Jericho remembered, his features crag-like, scarred. His steely blue eyes told a story of unfathomable depths.

Finally, Jericho spoke. 'Who are you?'

'Did I no' introduce myself the last time we met?'

'That wasn't real.'

Fillan arched an eyebrow. 'Was it no'?' he said. 'I presented ye with the opportunity to safeguard yer future, and did ye heed me?'

'That was a dream, and now I'm in the middle of another one—'

'Tell me, laddie, who will die when ye rouse yerself this time? Yer son, yer wee lassie?'

Jericho bunched his fists.

Sadness flickered in Fillan's eyes. 'No more running for the whisky, eh?'

'How do you know so much about me?'

'All in good time,' he said, his forefinger tracing the line of his lower lip. 'Years ago, I was a soldier. Found myself caught up in a rebellion. The English rounded us up. Executed the ringleaders. Deportation for the rest of us. Quebec—'

'You were in the forces? When was this?'

'It was '43. Aye, I fought for kith and kin. I had my wee lassie at home, two bairns. I escaped from London and made my way back home. When I arrived, I found the door open. My wife and children were gone. Redcoats, that was my first thought. I scoured the grounds for signs of their passage. No dragging of heels left in the mud. No human footprints. She'd have struggled, my Megan. Left her mark on someone. Puzzled, I traipsed the perimeter of the croft. A set of paw prints, big as a bear, ran anticlockwise from the front door in a complete circle.' He tapped a finger on his forehead. 'In my mind, I saw her. She heard a noise. Stepped outside—'

Fillan's tones were smooth. Jericho wondered how many times he'd told the story around a fireside. He glanced back at Birdy. She'd moved from the pond and stood ten feet away, unsure. 'And this bear got her?'

'No' a bear! I only said the prints were that size. It was a wolf.'

'How could that take a grown woman and two children?'

Sorrow filled Fillan's eyes. 'First, he killed her, then the bairns. Took them one by one to his lair.'

'I'm so sorry,' Jericho said. 'What did you do?'

'I went after him.'

127

'You catch him?'

'Aye, I found him, or rather, he found me.'

'He hunted you?'

'Let me finish, lad, then ye'll know.' He cleared his throat. 'Early November, and the air uncommonly warm, I remember squinting into the pale sunshine along a track I'd searched many times. The dogs caught the scent on the breeze and ran ahead. I followed up the rocky path. Couldn't see no tracks or droppings. Couldn't smell nought but the tang of salt blowing in from the coast. The trail grew steeper, winding around a corner up the crag. I shouted after them, What are you onto, a mountain goat? I called them back, but they wouldn't come.' Fillan paused and jerked a thumb at the pigeons gathered in the trees. 'Look at them. All plump and ready for the pot.'

'They found him?'

'No, but we couldn't climb any higher. The ground flattened out and ended with a rocky outcrop. I watched as the dogs disappeared into a cave. I charged after them. Sure enough, it was a wolf's lair. Inside were two cubs. Black as coal. I cut off their heads.' He scythed the air with the edge of his hand. 'Quick as ye like, and bagged them, for no one believed wolves still ran wild, and if ye had proof, there was a bounty. I had just finished, and the cave suddenly went dark. In the mouth of it, a she-wolf. Took her but a second to understand, and then she came at us, snarling, savage.'

'You and the two dogs would've made short work of her.'

'Short work? She nearly killed us all! When it was done, I saw human remains all over the cave. Chewed-up bones everywhere. At least twenty skulls. Then I found my

128

Megan's wood and silver crucifix.' Fillan stared into the distance. 'For what good it did her. It broke my heart to think the remains of all I knew and loved was strewn across that cold stone floor. I shouldn't have stayed a moment longer, but it didn't seem right to leave that God-forsaken place without a prayer for my family. There was justice in what I did. An eye for an eye. Another severed head added to the brace already strung over my shoulder, tongues a-lolling.' He inhaled long and hard. 'I walked out, looking for a place to ambush the male. If we were lucky, we'd catch our breath before he came. No such luck! He howled like he knew the sight which awaited him. Rabbits bolted for cover. The dogs bristled, uneasy. The sky darkened as even the sun hid away.'

Jericho glanced over his shoulder, half expecting the wolf to reappear. Birdy stood as if mesmerised.

'The air surrendered to an icy chill. A snowflake fell. A *skelf*. I knew then this was no ordinary wolf.'

Fillan's words rang a bell of truth. Jericho's doubts fell away. 'But you escaped?'

'Don't rush me, laddie. That wolf came out of nowhere. I expected him from below, but he came bursting out of the cave behind. Knocked me flat. My dogs come at him. I stuck him with my dagger like a madman. He's as big as a bear and black as night. Thick, thick mane. When I stared into those hate-filled eyes, my blood ran cold. The dogs came to my aid, although gravely injured. They were brave and loyal to the last. Without them, I'd have been finished, for he turned his attention to them. I could only watch as the beast tore them apart one by one. All that took less than a moment, and whilst I'd made it to my feet, I knew I'd not last a minute if he caught me again.'

'You stabbed him, and he still kept coming?'

129

'Aye, laddie. No stopping him. Locals talked long ago of a beast as old as the hills. A mob trapped it once, speared and clubbed it to death, but it came back to life. It was said the only way to kill it for good was to stab him in the eye. Anyway, I ran for the cliff. I'd seen how it lay on the climb up the path. If I made it over the edge and climbed down the sheer rock face, he couldn't follow. Fifty feet, then I could ride the scree.'

'You got away—?' Jericho stopped. He noticed a little wooden cross around Fillan's neck, a silver Jesus impaled upon it. He'd seen similar in the flea markets of Jerusalem, the wood purporting to be from the one true cross. 'You were in the Holy Land?'

'I'm no' here to swap stories.' Fillan switched his attention to the crane. 'If ye want to live, she's coming with me.'

'Is that a threat?'

Fillan laughed. 'No, lad. This ye must do to fulfil a prophecy.'

'She can't leave yet,' Jericho said.

The Highlander raised his eyebrows. 'Ye have no choice.' He clapped his hands. Branches previously laden with plum-grey birds emptied in a cacophony of beating wings as thousands of pigeons took off, heading east. Jericho gazed in awe. He turned to look for Birdy.

She and Fillan had gone.

Panicked, Jericho wheeled around full circle before looking up. On massive wings, she rose clear of the flock.

'No,' Jericho shouted frantically. 'You can't go yet!'

Higher and higher, she soared.

130

'Come back!' he cried, leaning back as far as he could. 'We never said goodbye.'

Birdy circled him in a wide arc at the top of the sky three times before breaking out and swooping after the dark specks flapping in the distance. He watched as she shrank further into the horizon and finally disappeared.

Chapter 25

Jericho turned to a new page in his journal. The action puffed air under the solitary fluffy white feather he'd found on the floor and kept on the table in front of him all day. It took off, rose a couple of inches, and settled again. He flexed his hand. It ached as much as the rest of his body. The unexpected departure of his beloved Birdy had made his punishing regime harder.

Fillan had mentioned '43. It was clear he meant 1743. If that were true, the Highlander was at least three hundred years old. Who, or what is he?

Jericho gave up trying to make sense of what was happening and slipped into simply recording the day's events as they unfolded. The pen ran out of ink. After finding another one in the drawer, he walked to the window to face his reflection in the dark glass.

Fillan hadn't given him much to help him track the wolf. *Near the coast.* He'd mentioned the tang of salt in the air. Clifftop. Steep winding path. Cave with multiple entry points. *It came from behind.* He could have just told him the location. Even if he found the lair, would it still be there? What the Highlander didn't have was google. Other than erosion, the land features in a remote place like that wouldn't have changed much.

He picked up the feather and carried it into the back room.

At his computer, he searched for caves on the Scottish coast. Massacre cave caught his eye. *Four hundred islanders murdered in a clan feud.* Interesting, but on the island of Eigg. Not what he sought.

Lossiemouth fit the bill perfectly, but the caves were under archaeological investigation. A place of human sacrifice throughout the ages. Could it be that the odour of decayed flesh and bones continued to draw wolves? Was it possible an undiscovered section remained? He read on. Grave goods. Charms and amulets. At least twenty-eight people died there. Children as young as two. What if the findings were wrong? Could a mutant variety of wolves have carried out the killings?

He continued. The Bone Cave. Remains unearthed of creatures extinct in the Highlands for thousands of years. Lynx, polar bear, arctic fox, lemmings. The disappearance of the land bridge between Scotland and northern Europe sealed the fate of those species. Whilst they thrived elsewhere, those trapped in the British Isles died out, never to return. Archaeologists also found human artefacts and evidence of wolves.

On and on, he read throughout the night. Occasionally, he paused, digesting the research before him. When was the last time his thoughts had gelled together so clearly? He learned people inhabited caves there until 1915, when the government made it illegal. He suspected that wouldn't be enough to keep those who'd forged a way of life outside the mainstream from clinging to the only existence they knew.

Jericho drifted into looking at ley lines, the connection between them and the old ways. All these things seemed somehow related.

He pined for his wife and children. For time lost. For the company of the majestic creature named Birdy. He'd seen something in her. Purity and innocence of the soul-cleansing kind.

Jericho wandered into the kitchen, straight to the cupboard containing the whisky. In a somnambulant daze, he reached for the bottle and, spinning off the cap, downed the contents at a tilt. Breathless and gravely disappointed in himself, he switched everything off and climbed the stairs. He swayed as he took Anita's favourite dress from her wardrobe, inhaled her perfume, and laid it on the bed beside him. 'I tried, Neet. I really tried,' he whispered and, closing his eyes, wept. Silently, he prayed for rest, but none came.

He glanced at his watch. Almost 3 am. Minutes turned into hours. Whatever experiences had occurred during the last three days, he doubted their reality now. He wasn't free. Not anywhere near. The truth, he concluded, had been an illusion concocted by despair. How much more of this can I take?

Like an automaton, he returned to the wardrobe, selected two ties, including the black one he'd worn at Anita's funeral, tied them together and formed a slipknot around his neck. He crouched, secured the loose end to the door handle and allowed his body to pitch forward, his knees a fulcrum, teeth clenched at the sudden overwhelming pressure on his windpipe.

What are you doing, you silly sod?

Neet, I'm coming home…

Flashes of his past life sprang from the well of his memory. The segue of images was too fast to latch onto. The storm ceased. Tears started from his eyes as they rolled upwards. He stared through the window into the night sky, silver stars winking in and out, transmitting some timeless code.

134

Chapter 26

Jericho's eyes snapped open. Daylight. Face down on the carpet, the noose still round his neck. Couldn't even get that right. Above the howling wind, he heard something. He worked the tie loose and removed it. Beyond the window, snow, driven horizontally, lent the illusion of his room first travelling backwards and then spinning out of control. Weary, unable to tell if this was a further delusion, he pinched his thigh, triggering a fleeting debate on the plausibility of waking oneself with pain. If the nip is real, am I not already awake?

Bang. Bang. Bang. A loose timber flapping in the wind?

He pushed himself into a crouch, head cocked, listening.

Bang. Bang.

Quieter than before, like knuckles rapping.

He grabbed his jeans and put them on while hopping towards the stairs. Who the hell can it be? In weather like this, the place is inaccessible.

Bang. The sound was now more muted.

'I'm coming,' he yelled.

Jericho wrenched open the door.

The woman leaning against it collapsed and fell backwards toward him. His hands shot out to catch her as she tumbled. 'I've got you,' he said, lowering her to the floor.

Her body was limp, and her eyes closed. Dressed in a white fur coat that perfectly matched her long hair, she was in her early thirties. Her beauty struck him. Pale skin, high cheekbones, full lips. He glanced at her bare feet and, gently patting her face, asked, 'Where did you come from?'

Beneath brows almost invisibly blonde, her eyelids fluttered, and when she opened them, he stared into them unashamedly. Blue-green and girdled in black, they flared with low spectrum changes the likes of which he'd never seen before. They settled on him. 'Where am I?'

'Miles from anywhere." Jericho looked at her feet, pink with cold. "What happened to your shoes?'

'I don't know…'

'I'll get you some socks,' he said.

'Could I have some water?'

'Yes, of course. Where are my manners?' He stood and offered his hand. 'I'm Jericho.'

She took it, and he hauled her up.

'You must be freezing. A hot drink would be better?'

She waved the suggestion off.

'Fair enough,' he said. 'Come through.'

She leaned on him as he led her into the lounge and sat her down. 'Your coat is wet. I'll take it, then get a fire going.'

'No.'

Jericho scratched his head. 'To the coat?'

'Yes.'

'Don't you want me to dry it?'

She squirmed. 'I've no clothes underneath.'

'What?'

She clasped her hands in her lap. 'I don't know where they are.'

'How did you get here? Sorry, I didn't catch your name?'

Small white teeth nibbled her lip. Her eyes widened. 'I can't remember it.'

'I'm not surprised. That cold out there is mind-numbing. You couldn't have been out there long, or you'd be frostbitten.' He gestured to her hands and feet. 'How do they feel?'

She flexed her fingers and toes. 'Tingly.'

'Not numb?'

Her head shook slowly.

'You're lucky. Another hour and you'd have been in real trouble. I didn't see a bag with you. How about a mobile?'

She looked puzzled. 'I don't have one.'

'Everyone has one of those. Is there anyone you want to call?'

'I can't think,' she said.

Jericho walked to the hearth, knelt, raked over the ashes and fired up some kindling in the grate. Then he arranged logs, criss-crossing them over the newborn flames. Where could she have come from? There are no other houses for miles. 'You must have been in a car,' he said, 'but even in a four-wheel drive, I can't imagine you'd have made it anywhere near in this deep snow. What happened? Did you crash?'

She shook her head. 'I honestly can't recall. Could I have that water, please?'

'Sorry, all this forgetting has got to me too! I have some clothes you can change into. Not mine. I kept them from… it doesn't matter. You're slimmer than she was, but I reckon you're about the same height.'

She smiled.

'I'll get the water and then sort you something to wear.'

Upstairs, he opened the doors to Anita's wardrobe. Inside, even after ten years, the scent of her perfume still lingered. He lifted the plastic covering to her favourite green and black dress, touched the soft fabric, and, gathering it into his hand, inhaled deeply. The first time she'd worn it, she smiled when he'd complimented her on how beautiful she looked. It took years before he finally refrained from laying it on the bed next to him at night. His new sobriety made him realise that *this* was the point when his drinking had worsened.

For a few moments, he lingered before his thoughts returned to the woman downstairs. There's no underwear for her, but nothing I can do about that. She'll have to make do with jeans and a baggy sweatshirt. He grabbed a pair of his socks from the airing cupboard.

If she didn't figure out who she was soon, he'd have to inform the authorities. Her family had to be worried about

138

her, but how would they get here to pick her up?

When Jericho returned with the clothes, she'd moved closer to the fire.

'You remembered anything yet?'

She shrugged. 'I'm sorry.'

'Don't apologise,' he said. 'We'll give it a while, then I'll phone the police to tell them I have you here.'

She nodded.

'Whatever happens, they'll have to wait for the storm to blow over. Not even a helicopter could reach us in these conditions.' Jericho put the clothing down on the coffee table. 'Best I could do. Change in there.' He pointed to the door leading into his study. 'You hungry?'

She picked up the clothes. 'Yes.'

'I'm not exactly spoiled for choice, so I hope you're not fussy. I'll get cooking while you make yourself comfortable.'

He switched on the cooker in the kitchen and watched as the halogen ring glowed orange beneath the glass hob. What the hell's going on? Is any of this real? Jericho neither knew nor cared anymore.

He was going with the flow.

Somehow, it seemed the right thing to do.

Chapter 27

Chantelle hovered close as Jack finished loading the dishwasher. 'It's a great idea, baby, but, and it is a big but–'

'It is not!' She turned sideways to strike a pose.

'You're sharp tonight,' he said, patting her bottom. 'I don't think I could stand Kurt over Christmas.'

'This is not about you, chéri.'

'I know, but still.'

Chantelle grabbed his hand and pulled him towards the couch. 'Talk to Emily. We watch the Revenant after, non?'

Jack scowled. 'After the nightmares it gave me? No thanks.'

'*Il n'y a de réalité que dans l'action.* There is no reality except in action, according to Sartre.'

'That's a long-winded way of telling me it's not real?'

'Isn't it so that we must face our demons?'

'Sartre said that?'

'No, somebody else.'

'Don't quote unless you know the source,' he said. 'Besides, it isn't my demon.'

'Keep it that way, please.'

'I'm going to call my sister, and then, against my better judgement, we'll put the movie on.'

***

Emily lounged on the sofa, feet up on the cushions, phone at her ear. 'I'd love to, although I doubt we could afford it, little bro. I'll talk to Kurt and get back to you, okay? Yes… bye.'

'What was that about?' Kurt lifted her legs and sat, resting them on his lap.

Emily blew out her cheeks with a deep sigh. 'Jack wants us to go to Scotland. To surprise Dad for Christmas.'

'Out of the bloody question,' he said hotly.

'That's it? Dismissed with no discussion?'

'We can't afford it, end of story.'

'It's about more than just money, Kurt.'

'Not to me, it isn't.'

'No, of course. Nothing else counts as long as you have money for your tinnies.' Emily swung her feet to the floor and stormed to the kitchen.

Kurt pushed off the settee and went after her. 'That's not bloody fair.'

Emily spun to face him, finger-pointing. 'It's all about you, isn't it?'

He tried to snatch her finger.

She jerked it away. 'Don't touch me!'

141

'Where's this coming from?'

'You!'

'Fair enough. You're worried about your dad, but his situation isn't my fault.'

'How long have we been engaged?'

'What?'

'How long?' she yelled.

'Almost ten years.' He paused. 'Is that what this is about?'

'No!' Emily cried. 'Yes! It's always been we can't afford to marry. I'm sick of hearing it.'

'Oh, Ems,' he said, shaking his head. 'I wanted to surprise you at Christmas by suggesting for our tenth anniversary–'

'What?'

'Let's get married next year.'

Emily slumped back against the counter. 'Is that why you said out of the question?'

'Yes,' he said and pulled her into a hug, whispering in her ear. 'That's if you'll still have me.'

***

'Your phone.' Chantelle paused the movie. 'Did you leave it in the bedroom?'

'How on earth did you hear it?' Jack scouted his immediate vicinity, making no effort to get up from the sofa. 'Yes, looks like it.'

'You want me to answer?' she said, already halfway across the room.

'Whoever it is, I'll call them back.'

'It might be Emily,' she said. 'I have not talked to her for ages.'

He channel-hopped while waiting for Chantelle to return. Finally, she emerged from the bedroom.

'Kurt says they cannot make it.'

'Yes.' Jack clenched his fists in jubilation.

'They are getting married.'

He dropped his hands. 'Oh, Christ! I thought she'd eventually come to her senses.'

'Love is blind. And the meat of one man is the poison for another, non?'

'Seriously, while I'm happy for her, I'm happier for us,' he said. 'Going to Dad's will be like a second honeymoon.'

'I will book the hotel in the morning. When will you tell your father?'

'I'll let Emily soften him with her news first…'

'We can go out to eat on Christmas Day?'

'I'm excited to see him already,' Jack said. 'And yes, of course we will.'

Chapter 28

The woman with no name had slept all day and now sat in an armchair by the fire. She said little, and Jericho knew no more about her than when she'd first arrived. In the fireside glow, she resembled a work in progress of some great painter, her face and hair as white as a blank canvas, outlines daubed with fiery yellows, reds and orange golds, framed for a moment in the kitchen hatch.

'Dinner is served,' he said, conscious of his lips sticking to his teeth. 'What can I get you to drink?'

'More water?'

'Nothing stronger?' The words slipped out before he could stop them.

'No thanks. I need to keep my wits about me.' She laughed. 'I already don't know who I am.'

Relief and disappointment flooded through him in equal measure. 'Then at least we have that much in common. Come through,' he said, turning away as she approached. He waited by the door to lead her to the dining room table.

She looked at the arrangement he'd put together. Neatly folded napkins, a lit candle in the centre and, on the plates, beans on toast.

A smile brightened her face, yet failed to mask her confusion. 'You shouldn't have gone to all this trouble.'

'No trouble at all.' He swaggered like a waiter, tea towel over his forearm as he waved her into the seat he'd drawn out for her. 'I'll get that water.'

What're you doing?

A new Jericho was in town and on an upward swing.

Jericho chatted easily with his guest over dinner. Telling her about his family, he mentioned nothing about himself or the events of the last few days.

'It's a funny thing,' he said. 'Your memory loss. It's quite selective or appears to be.'

'What do you mean?'

'You retained enough to hold a conversation.'

'It's going to come back,' she said with certainty.

'I just can't imagine what trauma could have triggered it.' Even when she frowned, he noticed how remarkably unlined and alabastrine her face seemed.

'Are you married?' he said.

Her lower lip pushed out. 'I can't think beyond an hour or two ago.'

'Forgive me,' he said. 'It's none of my business, but are you aware of what marriage is?'

She tilted her face, eyes locked on his. 'I think so?'

'You wear no jewellery. You have no bag or mobile phone. Did someone rob you?' He stroked his chin. 'Can I look at your fingers?'

She offered her hands without hesitation.

145

Jericho examined them. 'There's no sign you've ever worn rings, let alone a wedding band. No marks at all. Here you are, stuck with me until the storm passes.' He grinned. 'You could've done worse and ended up in the Bates Motel.'

She crooked an eyebrow.

'Not heard of it? It's an old film, so hardly surprising.' Jericho pointed to her plate. 'I'll take that, then show you the bathroom and fix you up with a bed for the night.'

'Thank you,' she said.

Upstairs, he ran the bath. 'I'll watch this for you while you choose an outfit for tomorrow. Your room is on the left as you go down the hall. I left some T-shirts out for you to wear in bed later.' Thought of her sleeping naked in the room next door flashed through his mind. He felt heat rise from the back of his neck and spread over his face. Jesus, I hope she didn't notice. He turned his back on her quickly and moved away. 'I'm going to let the police know I have you safe here. I'm sure someone's worried about where you are.'

'All right, thanks.'

Jericho took out his mobile. No signal, and the Wi-Fi indicator wasn't showing. 'Not again,' he said half-heartedly. At least the power was still on. His brow furrowed. What's that dripping noise? 'Oh, Christ! The bath!' He dashed in and turned off the taps, thankful he'd heard the overflow before it flooded everywhere. After mopping the floor with an old towel, he yelled, 'Bath's ready.'

Bare feet padded along the wooden floor as he walked downstairs. In his mind's eye, he again imagined her naked.

'If ever I needed a drink, it's now,' he muttered. Dragged by the lure of the bottle in his kitchen cupboard, he stared at the door. His hand stretched for the handle as if someone else controlled it. He squeezed his eyelids shut.

Don't give up, son. You've come this far.

A whiff of his father's cologne drifted into his nostrils, and he wheeled around to look for him. 'Dad?'

'Are you okay?' the woman asked.

Jarred from a moment he'd have liked to continue, Jericho rubbed two fingers against his left temple. 'I didn't hear you, sorry.' She wore Anita's favourite green and black floral dress by Laura Ashley. *Should I ask her to change? No, that would require an explanation. Leave it. It's not like I said, don't choose that one.*

'Are your parents alive?'

'Huh?' he said, struggling to stay focused. 'No, they died years ago.'

'Something reminded you of your father?'

'I'd forgotten how much I miss him–and Mum.' Jericho stared at the floor. 'Loneliness… it gets to me sometimes, that's all.'

'Whose clothes am I wearing?'

He looked up. Her eyes revealed she knew the answer.

'Why didn't you tell me?' she said, moving closer.

'That my wife died? I don't normally discuss it with strangers.'

'I'm sorry. It's just that I–when you open that closet–she doesn't seem far away.'

Jericho sighed. 'At first, I'd choose a different outfit and lay it beside me on the bed.' He glanced at her, afraid to make eye contact. 'Later, the one you're wearing became my favourite. I'd sleep with it there all night. Get up in the morning, smooth it down and put it away again. Isn't that crazy?'

She took his hand. 'I don't think so. It's hard to let go of someone you love.'

He pulled his fingers clear. 'What would you know about it? You don't even know who you are!'

'Not yet, but I can wait. How about you? How long will you wait before discovering who *you* are, Jericho?'

Chapter 29

In the lounge, Jericho lowered himself into an armchair opposite his guest. 'You warm enough?'

She popped open the top two buttons at the front of the dress. 'Much better, thank you. I've gone from one extreme to another.'

'The wind's died. It's the draft that makes the house so cold.' His eyes flicked over her newly exposed skin. 'Still not remembered your name?'

'No, but I had an inkling of something just now.'

'Like what?'

'I have a feeling I might have been a seamstress. A dressmaker. I'm not sure.' Her brow wrinkled. 'A weaver of fabrics, I think?'

Jericho nodded. 'Go on.'

'That's it. I can't remember anything else.'

'What kind of cloth?' he said. 'What dresses?'

'White...' She stared into the fire. 'Silk, perhaps?'

'Ballgowns?'

Her cheeks puffed out as she exhaled. 'Could be someone only showed me how to do it. Honestly, I do not know.'

'Come on, let's see if I can winkle some more out of you,' he said. 'It could lead to the return of your memory. How long ago would you say this lesson took place?'

'It isn't clear enough to put a time on it. I'm sorry.' Her eyes drifted to the horse brasses pinned to the oak mantle. 'That one there.' She pointed. 'See it? The third in.'

'That's a woman at a spinning wheel.'

'I think I used one of those before. And a loom.'

Jericho's brow furrowed. 'Do you think you're from a village community where they've kept traditions alive and taught them to children from a young age?'

She shrugged.

'Cottage industry is thriving these days,' he said. Outside, in his long barn, among the equipment left behind by previous owners, he recalled seeing an old still. He'd never fully explored what else lay concealed beneath the dust sheets, but he was sure there was a spinning wheel. 'These brasses depict country life as it was before the tractor age. There's a ploughman with his horses. A huntsman with his hounds. A harvester. Look, to be honest, I can't understand how you've kept your vocabulary and forgotten almost everything else.'

'I have a headache,' she said. 'Let's talk about you.'

'Discussing me won't get rid of it.'

'While you were clearing up, I read your journal.'

Jericho glared at her. 'I wish you hadn't. It's personal.'

'Some of what you wrote is disturbing. If you like, you can confide in me.'

'I don't know you!'

'Imagine I'm your oldest friend–'

'If you were, you'd know me already.'

'Jericho, it's the things you don't share that eat you up inside.'

He met her sympathetic smile with a tight one. 'Then that's how it is.'

'You're a kind man. You shouldn't punish yourself so.'

He got to his feet. 'Speaking of which, I'm behind on my exercise quota.'

Disappointment etched her tone. 'I'll leave you to it, then. Goodnight.' She rose from her chair and walked across the lounge to the door.

'Goodnight,' he said.

She lingered, half in and half out of the room, watching him.

After a few seconds, he turned away.

Jericho stayed up long after his guest had gone to bed. He recorded his journal entries in more detail than usual; he struggled to conclude them. She'd seemed to linger before going to her room. His pencil poised, he decided the moment was unworthy of record, but continued to think about it. Was she waiting for me to say or do something? Could saying goodnight have triggered part of her memory? The next words he wrote posed a further question. How could she have forgotten entirely who she is?

A message pinged on his mobile. He picked it up. Four signal bars and the time was almost two-thirty am. 'Emily, for God's sake, girl, text me at a reasonable hour on a

Sunday morning.' He read the message. *Hey, Dad, I wanted this to be the first thing you see when you wake up. Kurt and I are getting married next year! So excited! Chat tomo. Ems.*

'It is tomorrow,' he mumbled and typed out his response. *Congratulations. Talk later.*

He selected the browser button and typed *amnesia* into the search engine. A list of results appeared. Google never ceased to amaze him, but he remained wary of its sources. He clicked on *Psychology Today* and researched everything he could find. This led him to the dissociative variant of amnesia. Symptoms included forgetting personal information, family and friends. This is what she has. Next, he read about the causes. Past trauma, accidents, abuse, stress.

War.

Jericho realised he suffered from a form of it, too.

Hours passed. Still, he couldn't sleep. The possibility of the exercise before bed contributing to his problem occurred to him. No matter what time of day, he'd never had trouble sleeping after vigorous activities before. The body changes as one grows older, and he recognised that. Yet now, he seemed electrified, as though he could track the progress of individual blood cells in his veins. He had so much energy he thought he'd catch fire. Is this how people spontaneously combust? If someone took a photo of me now, the surge of power would surely show up on the exposure like a force field.

Maybe I just don't need the rest?

Or was it that freed from the soporific effects of alcohol, he was coming alive again?

The contrast between this moment and how he'd felt when Anita died struck him hard. He hadn't allowed time to grieve. Instead, he'd sunk deeper into an alcoholic haze. She wouldn't have liked it, he knew that, but he couldn't deal with it any other way. Jericho realised if it weren't for the kids, he'd have followed her.

The children had wanted him to see a counsellor. His pride wouldn't allow it. Guilt gave him another reason to bury himself. He tried not to think of his wife and drank more during the lonely evenings to ensure he didn't. Everything of hers, he put away.

Now this woman set him thinking of Anita again.

Jericho reached into his bedside cabinet drawer and fished out a silver chain threaded through a gold ring. It occurred to him he should give it to Emily. He opened the clasp with practised fingers, fastened the chain around his neck, lifted the wedding band to his lips, kissed it, and closed his eyes.

Anita waltzed into his consciousness.

'You can't keep away, can you?' he said.

She held out her hand.

He took it. 'Where are we going?'

'To where we started.' She broke free and laughed. 'Come on,' she said, running down a cliff path.

Jericho chased her, hearing the first drift of music from below. An asphalt track between rock and sand stretched as far as he could see. In the distance, the sun dipped, framing the outline of an old ship moored at the end of a pier. Streams of people filed onto it.

153

'Come on!' she cried, striding ahead of him. 'Or we won't get aboard.'

The Lady Savile. Their first date. Run aground in a storm, the owners sold her to a yacht club, turning it into a disco ship. Excitement brimming, they'd joined the queue. The attendant clipped the rope barrier into place. 'That's it,' he announced. 'No room for any more. Fire brigade rules.'

The music grew louder as they shuffled along the crowded pier. Jericho wrapped an arm around Anita's shoulder and kissed her. She shoved him away. 'What kind of girl do you think I am? Kissing in public!'

'I'm sorry.' he blustered, arms by his sides.

She grabbed him and pulled him back. 'I'm only kidding,' she said, her mouth finding his.

Inside, it was so loud they spoke into each other's ears and still couldn't hear. Jericho relayed Anita's order to the barman, pointing to the bottles. 'Beer and a gin and tonic,' he yelled just as the music switched tracks. The man laughed. 'No need to shout, mate!'

It seemed everyone on deck had turned to face him. He shrugged, paid and took their drinks up to the open-top deck. The breeze carried away the last of the day's warmth as they drank and talked and gazed over the shimmering sea until the sun faded and a sickle moon sailed in, sprinkling the gentle crests of the inky waters with silver.

They danced to Golden Oldies among the other couples in a world of their own, laughing at how the drum and bass-driven John Kongos' Tokoloshe Man translated into a pseudo hillbilly line dance. Jericho followed her lead. 'I feel ridiculous!' he said, a hand on her shoulder, the other clasping hers as they kicked their legs out, bending deep sidewards at the waist like human metronomes marking out time on a night he'd wished would go on forever.

Later, hand in hand, climbing the cliff path in the darkness, giddy with happiness, he told her he wanted to see her again.

'I haven't finished with you tonight yet.'

'I know,' he said.

'How do you know?'

He grinned. 'The song said, "When Tokoloshe says tonight is tonight, it's tonight."'

Anita smiled, perplexed. 'So, now we're doing what the lyrics say?'

The beat of music lodged in his brain, and he fell silent. The streetlights winding uphill bobbed with each step taken, like a procession of torches leading him into a long-buried darkness.

Jericho screamed.

A gentle knocking drew him back to the present.

'Jericho?'

Thick with emotion, his vocal cords refused to cooperate. 'Yes?' he said in little more than a hoarse whisper.

The door opened, casting a rectangle of light across the floor and up the bed. The young woman stepped into it. 'I heard you cry out. What's wrong?'

'Oh, God. Did I wake you? I'm so sorry.' She's still wearing Anita's dress. 'You not been in bed?'

155

'I couldn't sleep.' She took a couple of steps towards him.

'What're you doing?'

She smiled, soft and slow. 'I think I know my name.'

Jericho reached back and tugged the pillow higher to rest his head and see her better. 'I'm all ears.'

'Anoushka.'

'Really?'

Her eyes sparkled. 'Yes…'

'You're foreign?'

'Do I look it?'

He squinted at her. 'Russian?'

She laughed. 'I don't recall.'

'Anoushka isn't your name, is it?'

'I need to be someone,' she murmured. 'You need to call me something.'

Jericho scratched his cheek. 'All right, Anoushka, it is.'

'What were you dreaming about?'

'Nothing.'

'You screamed, you cried, and it was nothing?' She sat on the corner of his mattress. 'Jerry, talk to me.'

Her calling him Jerry rankled him. 'Please…' His foot shoved against her hip from under the duvet. 'Go back to bed.'

'Are you kicking me out?' Her teeth gleamed in the dim

light.

'There's no need for you to be here.'

She leaned over him, and her fingers brushed his neck. 'What's this?'

Horrified, he realised his botched attempt from a few hours before had left a mark on him. 'I tripped, caught it on the bedpost.'

'Let me look.'

Her face was inches from his. A hint of Anita's perfume drifted into his nostrils.

'It's nothing. Just go back to bed. We can talk in the morning.'

Squinting, she ducked to one side, allowing the light from the doorway to fall across him. She turned his chin and inspected the curvature of the bruising. 'Oh, Jerry…'

Naked and ashamed, his eyes met hers.

'I'm staying with you tonight,' she said.

'Don't…' he said, his voice tight.

She threw back the covers. A mischievous grin made her intentions clear.

He cupped his hands between his legs. 'I'm too old for you.'

'If I thought that, I wouldn't be here.'

His heartbeat rose steadily. 'It isn't right.'

Anoushka climbed in next to him.

'Oh no, you don't,' he said quietly. 'We don't want you

putting creases in that dress.'

'I'd best take it off then.' She smiled and pulled the garment over her head, tossing it over the curved brass rail at the foot of the bed.

Jericho marvelled at her nakedness in the grainy light.

She shook her long blonde hair, half-turning to glance at him as she lay down.

Her softness and the faint odour of Anita on her skin overcame him.

'Say my name,' she whispered.

Chapter 30

Traces of the night before lingered like the silken cobwebs of a beautiful dream. Jericho's arm circled the space beside him. Empty. No hint of warmth. Was she ever there? He cast his eyes to the corner of the bed. Anita's dress hung over the bedpost. A pang of something like regret rode his bright mood, turning it sour. Guilt for Anita and equally for himself. Why did I deny myself for so long?

A sweet melody drifted into his room, and with it, a rhythmic sound like tinkling bells.

Anoushka?

He rolled onto his side, winced at the stiffness in his lower back, and sat up. Pausing on the edge of the bed, he whispered. 'What were you thinking, old son?'

The soft thump of cupboard doors closing and the chink of plates reached him at the same time as cooking smells.

Would there be awkwardness over breakfast? Would she even acknowledge what happened? He got to his feet and dressed.

Wrapped in a white sheet, barefoot and light on her toes, Anoushka danced ladle in hand, tapping on pans, pots and cups while singing something folky.

Jericho watched, increasingly beguiled.

Her head turned as if suddenly aware of his presence. 'Hey.'

'Hey,' he replied. 'I see you've been busy.'

'I was up at first light. The storm had subsided, so I went for a little walk outside—'

'You can't do that,' he said, a sudden burst of anxiety flooding his senses.

She shrugged. 'Why ever not?'

'You read my journal. You saw there's been a wolf prowling around.'

'Yes, I just wasn't sure if you really believed it.'

'Well, despite my private ruminations, I do.'

'Oh, Jerry, I'm sorry.' She put a hand on his. 'I saw nothing on my walk?'

'I'll be back in a minute.' Jericho strode to the window and looked out. Repeated the procedure in each of the ground-floor rooms. When he returned, she'd laid breakfast on the table.

'See?' she said. 'I told you.'

'Well, he's out there. Somewhere.' It occurred to him he hadn't seen it since Birdy departed. 'How far out did you venture?'

She pointed west. 'Down to the edge of the woods. Around the perimeter fence. Peeked into your barns. I was outside for an hour.'

He glanced at her feet. 'You weren't barefoot?'

'No, I found some Wellington boots in the cupboard by

160

the door.'

'You must be exhausted after tramping around in two feet of snow?'

'And hungry.' She took a bite of her slice of toast. 'Come on, let's eat.'

'My daughter is getting married,' he said, covering his mouth to conceal the food he was chewing.

'You found out this morning?'

'Last night.'

Anoushka narrowed her eyes. 'You didn't mention it. Are you not excited about telling people?'

'It was just before you came to my room.'

'It's okay,' she said. 'I doubt I'd share the news with a stranger, either.'

'I guess that's why I'm telling you now.' He shifted in his chair. 'About last night.'

'What about it?'

There was an insouciance in her smile he found endearing, and it didn't help him express his thoughts freely. 'Someone, somewhere, is missing you. They must be. I need to do the right thing and tell the police you're here and you're okay.'

The smooth skin on her forehead furrowed. 'There's obviously no one important enough in my life to remember.'

'Nothing came back overnight?'

'No.'

'Parents, brothers or sisters?'

161

'I am alone, Jericho. Same as you.' She half-smiled. 'What unseen hand led me to your door, I do not know, but I'm glad.' She stood and ran her fingers through his hair. 'Can we go outside?'

'Let me grab my gun first.'

'When we return, I want to hear everything about you.'

She steered him towards the long barn. 'I thought I saw a loom through the window earlier.'

'I'm not sure what's in there exactly. Previous tenants moved on without clearing their shit. Those barn doors open out. We'll need a shovel to clear a way.' He slapped his forehead and pointed to the picket door. 'Wait, that opens inwards.' Finding the key on the cluster he carried with him, he unlocked it.

Inside, the grainy light penetrating the windows failed to illuminate the deepest recesses. The fluorescent tubes above popped and fizzed. Too high to tap them into life, they waited until the starters had warmed enough to kick in.

She pointed to the loom in the far corner, jutting out from a ragged dustsheet stacked behind a pile of equipment accumulated over a hundred years. 'There,' she said excitedly. 'I knew it.'

Jericho smiled in awe at her child-like enthusiasm. 'Are you sure you weren't a seamstress in another life?'

Anoushka bounced up and down on the spot, clapping her hands together. 'Can we get it out, Jerry?'

'Now?' He placed a hand on the small of his back and winced. 'After last night, I'm not sure…'

162

'Please?'

'It's probably broken, or the wood is rotten….'

A further glance at her pleading expression and he began clearing obstacles to reach the loom. 'I'm going to need my tools,' he said. 'If I dismantle it, we can reassemble it indoors, plus I can get a good look at anything that might need servicing.'

Chapter 31

Emily leaned back in her chair. 'Kurt, I asked for your opinion. I'm not interested in what your mates from the pub would make of it.'

He picked at the curved seam around the sofa's arm. 'In a roundabout way, that's what I was coming to. If this were a story in the papers, you and me, we'd have picked it apart, had a bloody good laugh exploring the ridiculous—'

Emily flushed. 'It's my dad! So, nothing to laugh at.'

'I realise that, but from what you and Jack said, and I'm not suggesting anyone is making anything up, there's a chance your father is suffering a confabulation.'

'Do you even know what the word means?'

He frowned, skirting the question. 'Let's work it out,' he said. 'What are the chances Jericho forgot about such an important event for ten years, only to recall it happening where he's living now? We all know he's had a problem with the old drinking—'

'Don't you dare!' Emily's eyes blazed. 'Yes, he likes a tipple, but Mum died right in front of him. It's no wonder he's struggling to make sense of it.'

He raised a hand. 'I didn't mean to offend you, Ems. When Jack goes over Christmas time, we'll know much more.'

She rose from her chair.

'You going to the kitchen?'

'Get it yourself,' she said over her shoulder.

'Aww, c'mon,' he said, changing the TV channel. Muay Thai music filled the room, and there was chaos of screeching pipes, drums, and cymbals as the combatants performed their individual versions of the *wai kru,* a ritual dance steeped in history. 'The fight's about to start.'

Emily joined him on the sofa with a beer for each of them.

Kurt opened his tin and took a deep swig. 'See that guy there in the black dragon pants? I can tell from his expression and pre-fight moves, he's gonna win.'

'I don't know?' She shook her head doubtfully.

'Am I ever wrong?'

Emily slapped his arm. 'Always,' she said, laughing. 'I'm saying the other guy. I love those gold shorts.'

Lips pressed into a thin line, Kurt refrained from comment, but his head turned left to right with exaggerated slowness.

The referee stood between the fighters at the centre of the ring, paused a moment, and then stepped back, signalling the start of the bout.

In the background, the crazy music began again.

Black dragon circled his opponent as the two engaged in a feeling-out process.

'He's gonna do him, Em.'

Gold shorts stamped his foot, feinted, and pushed down the right hand of black shorts. In a blur of motion, he spun around, his elbow connecting to the unprotected jaw of black shorts, dropping him instantly.

'Good night, *Irene,*' Emily whooped.

Kurt's mouth hung open, speechless.

As the evening wore on, they debated the merits of more fighters and placed further fun bets with each other. Kurt out-drank her by two to one, becoming more raucous with each swallow.

'Have you noticed how the music gets more frenzied the longer the fights go?' she said.

'That's the point of it,' he replied. 'To fire 'em up to keep bloody going, to try harder.'

'Why do they put themselves through such ordeals? That last guy's face looked like a tenderised steak, and still, he went the distance.'

Kurt shrugged. 'It's a question of honour, I guess–plus– the crowd loves it.'

'My Dad's changed,' she volunteered pensively.

'What's that got to do with muay Thai?'

'I think life's beaten him down to the point he can't come back.'

'Hey, listen, your dad's a fighter. He's gonna be fine. I'm always right, you know that...' Kurt sidled up and put an arm around her. 'The bloody world title is on the line here, Ems.'

She pulled away. 'You're so insensitive, you bastard,' she snapped. Perhaps that's one reason she felt attracted to him, he was similar to Jericho in this regard.

He paused the television. 'You okay?'

'Yeah,' she said, realising she was almost as good at hiding her feelings as her father.

Chapter 32

Jericho stood back and admired his handiwork. 'She's cleaned up really well,' he said, pointing to the loom.

Anoushka's eyes sparkled as she ran her fingers over the freshly varnished surfaces. 'All I need now is the finest white silk thread.'

'What will you make?'

She placed her forefinger on the tip of his nose. 'We shall see.'

'If you give me a list, I'll order whatever materials you need online.'

Anoushka came up behind him at the computer and rested a hand on his shoulder. 'How's it going?'

'That's all done for you,' he said, putting the list in the desk drawer. 'I don't know when it'll arrive. It depends on when all this snow melts.'

'As long as I have time to finish by spring.'

'You really have me intrigued. You must tell me.'

She turned his swivel chair to face her and sat on his lap. 'It's a surprise, and it's my secret....'

'I hope no one comes forward to claim you before I find out what it is,' he said.

'There's something else, Jerry. You cannot enter the room while I'm working, not even peep through the door.'

He laughed. 'Wow, it's top secret then.'

She leaned away to gaze into his eyes. 'I'm serious. If you do, I'll have to leave.'

He held her gaze for a moment. 'My God. You really mean it, don't you? I won't. You have my word.'

'Thank you,' she said and pecked him on the cheek. 'By the way, I'm yours. Nobody is coming for me.'

Jericho squeezed her knee. 'No one's said anything like that to me since my wife died.'

'Wouldn't it be funny if we had a double wedding with Emily?'

'What?'

'Don't worry, I'm joking,' she said.

He fell silent. What would the kids say?

'Penny for your thoughts?'

He smiled. 'You don't want to know what I'm thinking.'

Anoushka kissed him full on the mouth, rose from his lap and took his hand. 'I think I'm about to find out.'

Jack showered. Chantelle grinned outside, disrobed, and slid into the cubicle with him.

'Did you think any more about the visit to your father

over Christmas?'

Even after all this time, her glistening wet body still enthralled him. 'I struggle to think about anything but you when we're both naked and two feet apart....'

'Me, too, but we must decide.'

'Now Emily is getting married; it will stretch us financially.' He reached for her.

She put her hands out to fend him off. Despite the confined space and aided by the slipperiness of the soap, she easily outmanoeuvred him. 'First, we decide.'

'You're determined we should go?'

'It will be good for you to see him, chéri, non?'

His smile was broad. 'There goes my bonus.'

'We finish in here, then you call him.'

***

Jericho's phone buzzed on the bedside table before it rang. His eyes snapped open, and he reached across Anoushka. 'Sorry, Noush,' he said as she stirred, fumbling to pick it up. 'Hello?'

'Dad?'

'Yes, it's me.' He rolled over onto his back. 'To what do we owe the pleasure?'

'Chantelle is about to book tickets, but we thought we should run it past you first—'

'Run what past me?'

'We'd love to come to you for Christmas. Chantelle says she'll cook—'

170

'I'm sorry, boy, I've got plans.'

'More important than seeing me, us? What do you ever do, Dad, but refuse our invites? That's why we'll come to you.'

'It's not like that. You see, I'm in a new relationship—'

'What?' Jack paused. 'How did this come about? You said you were snowed in.'

Jericho chuckled. 'I can hardly believe it myself.'

'Dad–are you okay?'

'A million per cent. And guess what? I've given up the alcohol.'

'That's great. Perfect. Did she have something to do with it?'

'I haven't touched a drop since she arrived.'

'What's her name? Is she with you now?'

'It's Anoushka, and yes, she is,' Jericho said.

Jack took a deep breath. 'Can I talk to her?'

'She's sleeping, boy. Another time, eh?'

'So, it's a definite no to Christmas?'

'I don't want to put our new relationship under strain, sorry.'

'You heard that,' Jack said.

She rubbed his back. 'I'm sorry, chéri.'

'I'm half-inclined to go anyway, just to see if it's true.'

171

'He is your father,' she said. 'You must give him the benefit of the doubt, non?'

'He wouldn't put her on the phone. Made some half-ass excuse about her sleeping.'

She checked the time. 'It is early,' she conceded, 'but it is the new relationship....'

'Meaning?'

Chantelle winked at him.

'Ugh,' Jack said, scowling. 'I think I'm going to throw up.'

***

'You know, I think you're mean, Jerry,' Anoushka said. 'I'd have loved to talk to him.'

'It isn't so much that. Just that we don't know where you're from and how you ended up at my door. You know it would come up in conversation. Maybe not on the phone, but if Jack and Chantelle come at Christmas....'

'I'm sure they'd understand,' she said.

'Noush, it's done now.'

She lay staring at the shadows on the ceiling. The moonlight projected inside, sharpening the images so perfectly that she easily picked out the few withered leaves that clung to the skeletal branches. 'I love that you don't draw the curtains,' she said.

'There's no one outside to look in.' Flashback images of the wolf stole by. 'Not on this floor, anyway.'

'The downstairs ones are because of the wolf you saw?'

172

'Yes,' he said. 'I caught it looking in.'

She shivered. 'That's so horrible.'

'Can we change the subject?'

'I'm sorry, I didn't mean to remind you.' Her hand found his under the covers. 'You promised to tell me all about yourself.'

Jericho laughed. 'I don't remember that?'

'Don't forget your other promise,' she said. 'Now, tell me something I didn't read in your journal.'

'My mother didn't want me to join the army.'

Her fingers entwined with his. 'Carry on.'

'As far back as I can recall, all the Mathers' men served in the military. Mum was no shrinking violet. She'd seen what service did to my father.'

'What did it do?'

'I remember little about him except this one time.' His eyes grew distant. 'A funfair came to town when I was seven. Dad came home unexpectedly on leave. I look back now and see that, uncharacteristically, he made a big fuss of me. I never knew where I was with him. Either he was down and short-tempered or up so high it was scary.'

Anoushka rolled onto her side and propped herself on an elbow. 'Did they take you to the fair?'

Jericho found himself once more among the lights and cranky music. The scent of toffee apples, candyfloss, fried onions and hotdogs hung sweet and savoury in the air. And the laughter. Crazy laughter.

173

Dad suggested a ride on the ghost train. Mum said, 'You two go on. I'll be waiting around the other side.' He'd sensed his mother's fear, had seen it in her face and the way she'd emphatically shaken her head.

Led by a firm hand into the mouth of a cave, bats swirled around the ceiling, giant spiders ascending and descending threads, distant moans, a billowing wind, the gloom inside and then suddenly an explosion of bright lights and racket. Without warning, his father cowered, then dashed across the tracks into the nightmare landscape, dragging young Jericho behind. 'Come on, boy, we've got to get out of here.'

Angry shouts pursued them into a murky cavern, followed by a witch, two ghosts, and eventually a clown. The chase terrified him, but what he remembered most of all was the giant who stepped out of the shadows, an enormous fist crashing through the air, knocking his father out cold.

Anoushka cleared her throat, snapping him out of his reverie. 'Jerry, did they take you or not?'

'Yes, they did.'

'Are you okay?'

'I was trying to remember, that's all.'

'What else can you tell me about your father?'

'Nothing, really.'

'Don't close up on me, Jerry,' she implored.

'I'm not,' he said. 'That was the last time I saw him.'

'Did he leave?'

'It was as if he knew we'd never see each other again.' A

tear trickled from his eye. 'The attention he paid me and all that.' Jericho scrubbed the wetness from his face with both palms. 'He died in action, Noush.'

'And you went against your mother's wishes and joined the army, regardless?'

'It's weird, but the more she schooled me against it, the more determined I became. As soon as I was old enough, I left home.'

'And you ended up traumatised, just like him....'

'Maybe...' And suddenly he remembered how he had wanted Jack to join the army, and Anita had resisted. 'Jericho,' she said. 'I don't care how many generations of Mathers' men were soldiers. The army is not taking my son, not after what I saw it did to you....'

'What did it do?' he said aloud.

'You ended up traumatised, silly,' Anoushka said.

'Jesus, Neet, I forgot that, too.'

She shook him. 'Hey, come back to me.'

His eyelids fluttered, blinking rapidly. 'I'm okay,' he said through thin lips. 'I just need sleep.'

'Night, Jerry,' she whispered and kissed his mouth. 'I'm here if you need me.'

Jericho turned over, drew his legs up into a foetal position, and fell asleep within seconds.

Chapter 33

Suddenly aware her breathing was rapid, Chantelle opened her eyes. On edge and unsure of the cause, she took a deep breath and held it. In the silence, punctuated only by her heartbeat, Jack whimpered. His legs thrashed. Her thoughts, sluggish at first, cranked up full speed instantly. Mon Dieu, he is in the throes of another nightmare. Her elbow jabbed into his ribs. 'Jack,' she cried. 'Wake up!'

In shock, he threw himself out of bed, falling flat on the floor. She rolled over and peered down at him. 'Are you okay, chéri?'

'What does it look like?' he said, wild-eyed and confused.

'Come back to bed and tell me what happened.'

'I dreamt about that bloody wolf again. It trapped me. I couldn't get away, but then you woke me. How long did you leave it before waking me this time?'

The green digits of the bedside light flashed 2:07 am. 'As soon as I realised,' she said. 'Where did you see it?'

'Oh, God, babe. I saw it, and I tried to sneak away, but it sniffed the air and turned round. I was on top of a mountain, nowhere to run.' He blew out his cheeks. 'The only way was down. Too far to jump, I scrambled over the edge, dropping first to my elbows, watching it speed towards me. I got a footing, and no sooner had my hands left the ledge to start the descent than it snapped at where they'd been.'

'It could not follow you?'

'No, the drop was vertical. My hands and knees, already raw and bloodied from the ascent, barely functioned. I thought I'd slip at any moment, actually felt the anguish. I've never experienced dreams like this before, and it bothers me.'

'You had cheese before bed?'

'A tiny piece of cheddar.'

Her expression scolded him. 'So, then what happened?'

'I'd almost got to the base. I hung by my fingertips, ready to drop the last six feet. The area immediately below was clear of rocks or anything to twist my ankle, and then I saw it, crouched, ready to leap. That's when you woke me.'

'No more cheese before bed,' she said.

Jack searched her eyes. 'I think we both know this has nothing to do with what I eat before bed....'

'To say it is anything else means what? That it can infect dreams and bring about the terrors of the night? Because if that is what it is, how do you battle it? No, this is just what your father told you about, and now you regurgitate it in your subconscious.'

'If you believe that, why did you wake me straight away?'

'Half of me is not sure, and I do not want to take the chance.'

Chapter 34

Over breakfast, Anoushka questioned Jericho further. 'You tired quickly talking about your past, and I was thinking for ages while you slept.'

'Penny for your thoughts,' he said, winking.

'You slept really well, but then I guess that after the events of the last few days, you had to.'

'I just hit a wall. Too much happening all at once. I've opened up to you with things I hadn't thought of in years.'

'It clearly took its toll,' she said. 'Do you suffer from low self-esteem, Jerry?'

'Not at all. I put the needs of others before mine.'

'The question wasn't about selfishness…'

For a moment, he hesitated. 'Why would you ask that?'

'People of your generation with post-traumatic stress disorder don't show they're sick. They fake being well.'

'I'm *not* sick,' he said.

Anoushka looked him in the eye, pursed her lips and shook her head slowly. 'It's nothing to be ashamed of.'

Jericho thought about it. 'I was drinking a bit,' he conceded.

'Okay,' she said, leaning back. 'I'm going to ask you for another promise.'

'What's that?' he said.

Although she smiled, her tone was serious. 'No more drinking.'

He nodded. 'Yes, all right, it's a deal. Something bothers me, though.'

She arched an eyebrow. 'Yes?'

'How you seem to know so much about me?'

'You're an open book, Jerry.'

Jericho held onto his chest, looking panic-stricken.

'Whatever is wrong?'

He glanced at the clock. 9:07 am. 'Just felt really jittery for a moment.' He inhaled deeply before letting his breath out slowly. 'Don't know what that was all about?'

'Perhaps skip the exercises today?'

'It's nothing to do with exertion or needing a rest. Besides, I lost my way and found myself through physical punishment. I'll let breakfast settle, and then I'm back to it.'

'You know best,' she said.

'Afterwards, I'd like a demonstration of the loom in action.'

She smiled. 'Sure, do you have any thread?'

'So, you remember how to use it?'

'I'm not sure it's a memory thing. It's automatic, like breathing. You just know, you know?'

Two days later, there was a knock at the door. The sound of a diesel engine chugging away out of sight on the driveway. Jericho recognised the man as Bates, a farmer from town. 'I'm doing the rounds on my tractor. Can't get to town any other way. Is there anything you'd like brought back?'

'I'm good for supplies, but could I ask you to check the post office and see if they have some parcels for me?'

'Sure, no problem.'

Later, Bates returned with the packages. Jericho peeled off a twenty-pound note from his pocket and thanked him. 'Is that enough?'

'I'd have done it for nothing,' the farmer told him.

'Noush,' he yelled. 'Your order's here,'

Keen to get started, she unboxed everything and set to work. 'No peeking,' she reminded him.

Anoushka disappeared into the room and closed the door. Save for her whistling a strange tune, the only sounds were the creak and thud of the timber mechanism he recognised from the demonstration she'd given him.

Once he'd finished his workout and showered, he nearly forgot his promise not to go in. Anoushka had further elaborated on her conditions of work before shutting herself away. *I'm taking in everything I need. I don't want any disturbances at all.*

Jericho kept himself busy with his journal until supper time, at which point he almost knocked to ask what she'd like. At the door, he listened intently to the scrape and clunk of the loom, her feet unrelentingly keeping a metronomic

180

rhythm. How on earth does she do this hour after hour?

Finally, at midnight, she joined him in the lounge. She was barefoot, he noted. 'My God, you look exhausted....'

'I'm okay,' she said, her smile wan.

'How's it going, Noush? I left you something to eat in the oven.'

'Oh, that's sweet of you, but I snacked steadily throughout the day.' She flopped onto the arm of the chair next to him and, lifting her legs one at a time, rubbed her feet. 'Gosh, I think I may have overdone it.'

'Let me do that for you,' he said.

'They feel icky, so I'll have a bath before anything else.'

Jericho got to his feet. 'You stay there. I'll go run it for you.'

When he came back down, she'd curled up and fallen asleep. Carefully, he scooped her into his arms and carried her upstairs to the bathroom. 'Will you be okay in the bath, or would you like some help?'

'No, leave me, Jerry. I'll be much quicker on my own.'

'Sure,' he said and left her to it.

He removed the meal from the oven and slid the contents into the waste bin. For a second, he considered sneaking down to see what she was working on.

The bathroom unlocked, and he heard her padding along the upstairs hall. Instead of her footsteps gently thudding in his bedroom directly above, the door to the spare room opened and closed. Not even a good night? The poor thing, she's absolutely drained.

Later, while waiting for sleep, he put together all the materials he'd purchased for her in his mind. Needles. White silk thread. He recalled their conversation from a few days earlier. *I might have been a dressmaker. What kind of cloth? White. Silk. Ballgowns?*

Wouldn't it be funny if we had a double wedding?

His heart kicked with excitement. My God. She's making a wedding dress.

Chapter 35

'There's much more to Dad's state of mind than just he lost my mum,' Jack said.

Chantelle nodded. 'Was he still in the army when they married?'

'Yes, he was.'

'Why did he leave the forces?'

'Mum always said he did it for the love of us kids and her, of course. Somehow, I don't think so.'

'I wish I had met her, chéri.'

'Yes, she'd have adored you. What a shame we didn't know each other before Mum died.' Jack closed his eyes for a moment. 'Probably better you didn't. Oh, my God. The day of the funeral was bad enough, but Dad made it worse by getting so drunk at the wake that one of his old army pals had to take charge of him.'

'Does he have many friends?'

'I don't think so,' he said. 'He never spoke of them if he did, but I just remembered the guy who helped gave me his card. If I can find it, maybe he can shed some light on Dad's trauma?'

'Good idea,' she said. 'I wonder if you will remember where you put it?'

'This'll surprise you, babe.'

She raised her eyebrows. 'It will?'

'Yes, it's in the box of my mum's memories, along with her funeral service pamphlet.'

Together, they strolled to the bedroom. Jack took the carton from the top shelf of the wardrobe. 'I haven't opened this since she died,' he said and, taking a deep breath, lifted the lid. 'I'm not sure I'm ready for this. Would you find it for me?'

She placed the container on the bed and sifted through the contents, pausing over a photo of Anita's wedding day. Jericho in uniform, ramrod straight, the two of them smiling at the cameraman. She opened her mouth to speak and decided against it.

Jack stood looking out the window.

Inside the Celebration of Life booklet, she found the business card Jack mentioned. *Robert Blake. Security Consultant.*

Chantelle held it out. 'It is here,' she said. 'You will call him, non?'

Jack walked over to her, took the card, and fished his phone from his pocket. 'Here goes nothing.' He dialled the number and put the phone on loudspeaker.

'Blake Security.' The voice was terse.

'Robert Blake? It's Jack, Jericho Mathers' son.'

'Oh, God.' A brief silence followed. 'He isn't dead, is he?'

'No,' Jack said. 'Nothing like that.'

'It's strange. I just walked through the door having attended the funeral of another of our colleagues.' The relief in his tone was palpable. 'Jerry's alive, you say? That means he and I are the last members of our troop still standing. I assume he's in good health? Last time I saw him, he got himself into a right old state.'

'At my mum's funeral,' Jack said. 'But is he okay? Now there's a question. It's why I called, really.'

'Go on,' Blake said.

'Obviously, he didn't react well to Mum's death, and he's worsened lately. My sister and I wondered if there's anything in his background that might have impacted him?'

'Did you say anything?' Blake whistled low down the line. 'I would say *everything*.'

'Can you give us a clue?'

'Our missions were classified. I'm not at liberty to divulge details. I'm sorry.'

'The rest of your squad, troop, whatever you called it. Can I just ask if any of those men exhibited unusual behaviours?'

Blake laughed. 'All of them. Why do you ask?'

'Dad seems to be losing his mind….'

Blake exhaled loudly. 'Tell me about it.'

When Jack had finished, Blake said, 'I tried to visit Jerry on my next leave after the funeral, but he'd moved away without leaving a forwarding address. The telephone number I had no longer worked, so naturally, we lost touch. You need to have a conversation with your father. Tell him you spoke to me, and he might open up. You understand, in this

185

case, it must come from him?'

'Of course.' Jack said.

'Would you give me your father's number?'

'I'll text it to you. If you get through to him, would you let me know how it goes?'

'Definitely,' Blake said.

'Is it me, or was that guy cagey, babe?'

She laughed. 'It is the code of silence, non?'

'I think if he talks to Dad, some good may come of it.'

'C'est possible,' she said. 'Especially if they meet. This Blake talks with his feet on the ground.'

'How long have you spoken English? I love the way you talk. It's so cute.' He reached for her hand. She welcomed him with open fingers. For a moment, they entwined. Jack disengaged, then pushed the keys on his mobile, the dial tone loud and clear on speakerphone.

'Who are you calling, chéri?'

He put a finger to his lips.

'Hey, little brother.'

'Hi, sis, how are you?'

Emily sighed. 'I'm bloody knackered.'

'Not sleeping or working too hard?'

'Probably both,' she said. 'Remember when you call, I'm eighteen hours ahead of you?'

Jack checked his watch. 'You're on your break, though?'

'Yeah, just saying.'

'I called an old army pal of Dad's. Remember the guy at the funeral who took care of him—'

She whistled. 'Yeah, he had the patience of a saint. What did he say?'

'Not a lot. Told me the stuff they did was classified, and I needed to talk to Dad if I needed to learn more, but he said he'd lost touch and wanted to call him, anyway. Agreed to let me know how it goes....'

'Good move, bro. Any other news?'

'Not really.'

Chantelle waved for his attention. 'Ask if she has the nightmares?' she whispered.

'Sis...?'

'Yeah? Spit it out, for Christ's sake.'

'I've been having bad dreams....'

'You too? That's why I'm so tired. Scared to go to sleep, and when I do, I mean, Kurt says I'm going bloody crazy.'

Staring wide-eyed at Jack, Chantelle slowly mouthed, 'Ask what she dreams of?'

'Don't keep me in suspense,' he mumbled. 'What are they about?'

'Ever since you told me of Dad's dream, I keep having it.'

'I should've kept it to myself,' he said.

'What do you mean?' A bell sounded in the background. 'I must go. That's the end of my break.'

'Okay, but you'd better tell Kurt we're both crazy….'

The call ended as abruptly as if the line were cut.

Chapter 36

Anoushka's dedication to her project astounded him. 'I'm not sure you need to slog every hour under the sun, Noush.'

'Now I've seen what I can accomplish in a couple of days, I'll pace myself better.'

'You still look tired to me,' he said. 'Maybe work alternate days?'

'Of course. I now know I need a certain amount of time to recuperate.'

'Whatever it is, there's no need to kill yourself. Spring is still a long way off.'

'That's true, but it'll be here before we know it.'

'Is it something for Emily's wedding?'

'You're close. Like I said, it's a secret.'

His breathing became more rapid, and his face flushed at the question he knew he had to ask. The thought was in motion, and he couldn't stop, no matter how crazy it seemed. Crazy had become a part of his life lately. He inhaled deeply.

Anoushka was already looking at him expectantly.

'Faint heart never won a lady, and I know we've only just met, but I feel like I've known you all my life, and—'

She took a step forward and put a finger to his lips. 'I thought you'd never ask.'

'Next year?'

'Could we do it the day after Emily and Kurt's wedding in Australia? Everyone who matters to you will already be there.'

'That's a great idea. I mean, it won't steal anything from their big day. We just have to tell them to make sure they don't go off on honeymoon straight away.' Thoughtful, he ran a finger over his moustache. 'I'll buy you an engagement ring as soon as we can get out.'

She waved him off. 'No need. I'm not going anywhere.'

Later that morning, while emptying the wash basket, he noticed a few blood spots on her jeans. 'Did you cut yourself working yesterday?'

'Oh, that,' she said, 'I pricked my finger. Isn't it amazing how much you bleed from such a tiny hole?'

'I'll get you some thimbles.'

'Jerry, honestly, there's no need. And from now on, you let me do the laundry.'

'I can't do that, Noush. It's a habit for me now.'

'Really,' she said. 'It's no trouble. I'll do it as soon as I've washed in the evening.'

Jericho shrugged. 'If you insist.'

The following night, once she'd finished her work and bathed, she lay with her legs across his lap while he stroked her aching limbs.

Her eyelids fluttered dreamily. 'Stop looking at my feet,'

she mumbled.

'I wasn't,' he said. His hand drifted from shin to ankle.

'Don't touch them either,' she said.

'I won't, but what's the problem with them?'

'They're ugly.'

'They're beautiful....'

'Didn't I just say don't look at them!'

Jericho couldn't tell if her irritation was real.

Moments later, she fell asleep.

His hands passed gently over her silky skin, feeling the fine, downy hair on her legs as he moved them to her feet.

On duty in China, he'd once touched the previously bound foot of a young woman. Although nothing like it in appearance, Anoushka's reminded him of hers, like bones scrunched into a shoe too tight for her.

'Gerroff,' she murmured without waking and pushed his hands away.

Reluctant to disturb her, he closed his eyelids and plunged into the dark void of dreamless sleep.

Jericho opened his eyes to daylight, still sitting on the couch. From the kitchen, Anoushka sang softly as the boiling kettle threatened to drown her voice. He stood, stretching his arms and stiff back.

The telephone rang. He stooped to pick it up. At this time of the morning, it could only be Emily.

'Hi, Ems. Are you okay?'

A gruff voice throat cleared. 'I'm fine, Jerry. And you?'

Jericho paused, sure he'd heard the voice before. 'Who is this?'

'It's been ten years, old son, but I'm still hurt you don't recognise me.'

'Blake?' he said incredulously. 'Is it really you?'

'Indeed it is,' Blake said. 'I'm pissed that you never sent me your contact details.'

Anoushka appeared in the doorway, her hands mimed eating with a knife and fork.

Jericho spread his fingers. *Give me five.*

'How did you find me?'

'Your boy called me. Asking questions.'

'About what?'

'About our time in the army….'

Jericho hesitated. 'I don't talk about that.'

'None of us did,' Blake replied. 'It's just you and me now, Jerry. Are we going to have a drink together before we die?'

'I just proposed to my girlfriend,' Jericho said.

'Am I invited to the wedding?'

'I feel you should be, but I recall little about you….'

'We need to meet face to face, old son. There's a lot to talk about.'

Ahead of him, a path meandered uphill into the darkness. 'Blake, I'm not ready. So don't call me. I'll call you.' He disconnected.

Christmas came. Jack and Emma called. After exchanging good wishes, both tried to speak with Anoushka, and Jericho made excuses each time. 'You'll meet her soon enough,' he said. In truth, he was still uncomfortable about how they'd react when they saw how young she looked. That's a bridge we'll cross when we get to it, he told himself.

Meanwhile, hollow-eyed and thin, Anoushka persevered with her task. Twice, Jericho ordered more silk. Concerned for her health, he ensured the silk wouldn't arrive until the New Year. While waiting, she returned to her old self. They sat together in the conservatory, observing the stars.

'How much more to go, Noush?'

'I'm a third the way through or thereabouts,' she said.

'But it's making you ill.'

She nodded. 'I knew I'd have to put a little more into it than I can afford, but it's okay. Not too long now.'

'That's the trouble with commitment,' he said. 'Especially what you're doing, pouring your heart and soul into it.'

From the corner of his eye, he spotted movement. Here in the wilds, it usually turned out to be a mouse, and he'd see the evidence of its presence the following day. Unusual to catch them on the move, but this one was white and rolled like a tumbleweed in the breeze. He bent to catch it. Curled-up and downy, it was a feather like the keepsake he had from Birdy. However, this one possessed a bloody tip. Must have blown in from outside, he reasoned. The remnants of a hawk attack.

Chapter 37

18th March 2018.

The night before, Anoushka told him she'd finish today. Jericho grinned. 'I've got a bottle of champagne I saved for a special occasion somewhere.'

'You don't drink,' she said. 'Let's take it with us to Australia.'

'Let me know in the morning as soon as you're done.'

Over breakfast, he suggested they celebrate with lunch in town.

'I'm not sure if I'll be up to it, Jerry.'

'Tomorrow then?'

She nodded. 'Yes, I should be fine by then.'

His curiosity was at a fever pitch; even his exercise couldn't distract him. By midmorning, he tiptoed to the workroom and listened. The thud and creak of the loom had ceased the day before. Still, she whistled her strange tune. The tear and snap of parcel tape against a cardboard box from the dispenser he bought her told him she'd finished. Then he heard her mumbling. As he leaned closer to the door, his head touched it. To his horror, it was unlatched and swung slowly open. He snatched at the handle and missed, his fingertips adding further momentum.

Naked, with a smattering of bloodied feathers underfoot, her chest red and blotchy, Anoushka stood tall and faced him.

'What are you doing?' Horrified, Jericho glanced at the plumage on the floor, his eyes roving her body uncomprehending. 'You've hurt yourself. Why are you working without wearing clothes?'

She covered her breasts. 'Oh, Jerry,' she said, her voice etched with disappointment. 'I told you what would happen if you came in.'

A sense of panic swept through him as he recalled her warning. 'Wait, I didn't. I wasn't... The door opened by itself—'

'A promise is a promise,' she said. 'Now I have to leave—'

'No, you can't go. You *must* believe me,' he pleaded, his fingers interlaced as if he were about to pray.

'I can't change the rules, Jerry.' She rushed to the French doors, turned the key and dashed outside.

The speed at which she moved caught him by surprise. He slipped on some feathers as he gave chase. 'No, no, Noush, wait. It wasn't my fault.'

Too late to stop her, she hopped, skipped and leapt into the air. Her skin turned white, great wings spread from her shoulders, the wind getting beneath them as she transformed into a white crane.

'What in heaven's name?' he whispered. 'Birdy?'

Dumfounded, Jericho followed her progress upwards.

She circled above him in a wide arc, high above, looking down. Heavy-hearted, he waved a last wave; she traced a final circle in the sky and then was gone.

Chapter 38

19th March, Calgary.

'You told your father we are coming, non?'

'I reminded him yesterday, babe.'

'What did he say? Is he looking forward?'

'He didn't answer, so I left a message on his answerphone.'

'And he does not reply?'

After his father refused the Christmas visit, Jack, in his wisdom, hadn't told him they were coming at all. Jack shrugged. 'You know what he's like.'

'You have the tickets and everything?'

Jack patted the breast pocket of his jacket. 'You ready?'

'Just the luggage to load up, and we go. I am looking forward to meeting Anoushka. Is she Russian?'

'It's a Russian name, for sure. He never actually said.'

She grinned. 'We will soon find out all about her.'

Jack's mobile rang. 'Jack Mathers,' he said, phone held in the cleft of his neck, manoeuvring cases through the front door.

'Mr Blake, we're just leaving to catch a flight. Did you talk to Dad?'

Chantelle gave him a querulous glance.

'Hang on...' He put the cases down. 'I'll put you on speaker, then I can talk and carry my luggage... that's better. You're in my pocket. Can you hear me?'

'Loud and clear,' Blake said. 'I'm sorry I've not got back before. I've been away the last couple of months, but I spoke to your father. Did you have that conversation with him?'

'No, he's been a bit evasive lately....'

'Tell me about it. I'm waiting for him to call me for a catchup.'

'I got a prediction for you, Mr Blake. Don't hold your breath.'

Blake laughed. 'I can wait. Do me a favour, though?'

'What's that?' Jack popped open the trunk.

'Tip me off where and when he's tying the knot.'

Chantelle's eyes widened.

'Who, Dad?'

'Who else?'

'Did he tell you he's getting married?'

'Of course.' Blake paused. 'He did tell you, didn't he, Jack?'

'The fuck he did.'

'Do me another favour,' Blake said. 'Don't tell Jerry I told you.'

Chapter 39

Fillan scratched his ear. 'All the things ye took for granted, ye see their value when they're gone.'

Images of Anita, Birdy and Anoushka bloomed briefly before him. 'You came here to taunt me?'

'No,' Fillan said. 'Just giving ye lessons in life. Ye never heeded my warnings, but I suspect ye'll listen now.'

'I'm all ears,' Jericho said.

'This house was once *my* house.' Fillan's hand swept across the frontage of the building. 'Not as ye see it now, of course. Mine vanished into the earth more years ago than ye can count.' His eyes scanned the horizon. 'Captured between the here and there for all time and him too. Now you and soon your bairns....'

'I already lost my wife. What does this have to do with my kids and me?'

Fillan rubbed his eye with the knuckle of his index finger. ''Tis a family curse, lad. Did I no' tell ye?'

Jericho covered his face with his hands. After a moment, he peered out. 'What are you saying?'

'The name's Fillan. Fillan Mathers—'

'Then why the hell didn't you tell me this before?'

'Ye kept interrupting me, lad, remember?' Fillan said through discoloured teeth.

'Oh. Now it all makes sense,' he sneered. 'So how come it got my wife? She wasn't a Mathers.'

'Ye let him into a door in yer mind. He infected yer dreams.'

Jericho knew he had closed that door too late, and now Jack had seen the wolf in his nightmares, too. 'How do I stop him?'

'None of this will end until ye kill him. Ye must do this on *Alban Eiler* before nightfall when the hours of the day match those of the night when all powers are equal. Here, lad, take this.' He handed Jericho a map. 'This is where he exists in the flesh.'

'I don't understand. So, what I saw when he attacked–it wasn't real?'

'He is freed with the snaw on the Day of the Dead. 'Tis when he's strongest. Ye stole the bird from him. If ye hadn't, ye'd no' be here now—'

'What?'

'He'd have had ye for sure. If he does no' feed, he fades back into the realm of darkness.' Fillan stroked his beard. 'I'd have killed him long ago, but I canna be in the same time and place as him. Kill him, lad. Set us free.'

'One question?'

'Aye?'

'If it killed all your family, how was the curse passed on to me?'

'I had a bastard son…' Fillan replied.

202

'Figures,' Jericho said.

That night, with diligence, he recorded everything in his journal. Before he left Fillan, the highlander explained precisely how to reach the wolf's lair. 'And ye must do it the way I did. On foot. Twenty-five miles over rough terrain.'

'Are you sure this will work?'

'You'd better hope that fate is on your side.' Fillan had said grimly.

Jericho googled *Alban Eiler*. The spring equinox. March 20th.

If he left in the morning, he'd be there in two days. In his journal, he wrote: *Aim to be there at 4:15 pm. It must be before sunset.*

Next, he looked up the area. Save for the addition of a few roads, the map seemed a fair representation of where he needed to be. He jotted the coordinates into the notebook. The map, he memorised, folded and slid between the pages in case he didn't return, figuring it lent some authenticity to the whole fantastic tale.

Before turning in for the night, he researched the wolf. Could it be that it had appeared in myth or legend?

Then he found a reference to a black wolf. Traditionally cited as the last in Scotland, and allegedly killed on the river Findhorn, between Fi-Giuthas and Pall-a-chrocain, in 1743.

The man who claimed to have done it wasn't Fillan.

Tomorrow, just as Fillan wore Megan's cross, he would wear something of Anita's and Birdy's. A wedding ring and a downy feather. Bound together with silver wire and worn

203

like amulets around his neck.

Chapter 40

Northwest Scotland 20th March 2018.

Chantelle snapped a picture through the car window. 'This landscape *c'est magnifique.* I can see why your father lives in these wilds.'

'It's a bonus, but I'm sure he didn't do it for the views,' Jack said.

She turned her gaze to him. 'Because he wanted to be alone?'

'Could be,' he said. 'There's a lot about him I don't understand. Probably never will.'

She nudged his elbow to make room for hers on the armrest. 'By the time our visit ends, you will know him better, chéri.'

'Possibly.' Jack glanced in the rearview mirror. 'I haven't seen another vehicle since we turned onto this road. Are you sure this is the right way?'

'One million per cent.'

He laughed. 'Pretty sure, then?'

'Of course. Like I knew you'd change the subject.'

The SatNav cut in. *In a quarter of a mile, turn left.*

Jack tapped the screen. 'How much further to the house?'

She leaned forward and squinted. 'It says twelve miles. The last section of the road looks like a track.'

'Glad we hired a four-wheel drive, then.' Jack flipped the indicator.

An hour later, they lurched through a dark wooded section before emerging at a meadow's edge. The sky grew leaden. A few flakes of snow dusted the windscreen, activating the wipers. She shivered. 'Did I not say earlier it feels cold enough to snow?'

'It's a few flakes, that's all.'

Her finger shot to the right. 'There it is, coming up.'

Jack took in the red-tiled roof and black weather-boarded walls. 'Just how I imagined it to be.'

They pulled up behind Jericho's car.

'No sign of life,' she said, peering at the house. 'I would have thought he would watch for us.' She glanced at Jack. 'Why do you look so terrified?'

His smile was thin. 'No reason. Come on, let's knock at the door.'

'You told him we were coming, non?'

Jack sighed. 'No, but he's going to be here.'

'You said he does not like the surprises.'

Jack switched off the ignition, got out, and strode up to the front door with Chantelle close behind.

'I hope this doesn't put him in a bad mood,' she said.

'He'll be fine,' Jack said, tight-lipped. He took a deep breath, raised the knocker, and let it fall. A moment passed. They looked at each other. Chantelle shuffled her feet.

His left ear turned towards the house, he listened carefully, then knocked again.

'He isn't here, Jack.'

'Could be in the toilet?' His eyes confirmed the lack of conviction in his voice.

Chantelle shook her head. 'And where is his woman?'

He shrugged. 'Could be out for a walk together?'

She walked down the side of the house. 'Maybe they go hunting?'

Jack followed, his mobile in his hand. 'It's out of season. Look, they can't have gone far. I'll call him.'

'Listen,' she said. 'I hear a cell phone ringing.'

Jack disconnected. The sound stopped. 'That proves it,' he said. 'They went for a walk or something.'

Snow dusted their hair and clothing. Chantelle zipped up her coat and stamped her feet. 'Let's have a look around. I'm getting cold.'

They traipsed the perimeter of the house, stopping at each window, hands cupped to see inside better.

She turned her nose up at the untidiness inside. 'This Anoushka… she is not good around the house.'

He nudged her ribs with his elbow. 'Well, you're here for a few days.'

'I am sure he is happy with things how they are…' she

said. 'Oh, look. I love that fireplace. Can you imagine how cosy it looks when it is ablaze?'

Jack stared at the burnt-out charcoal. Wouldn't he have left the fire burning?

'I wonder how his French is coming along?' she said.

'No idea...' Jack pointed to the French doors. 'Voila,' he said. 'Something to remind you of home.'

She slapped his shoulder and stepped close, her lips brushing his neck. 'Remember how I taught you le Français?'

'Baby, how could I forget?'

Her hand found its way inside his jacket and tugged on his belt. His stomach contracted. He nibbled her earlobe.

She pulled away. 'Wait.'

'What's wrong?' He followed her gaze to the deep gouges in the doors. Jack approached the marks. 'Dad said nothing about having a cat.'

She joined him, dropping to one knee. 'Whatever did this is much bigger, more like the lion,' she said. Her nose crinkled. 'Do you smell that?'

Together, they scanned a rapidly whitening horizon. 'Come on,' Jack said. 'Let's wait in the car.'

Jack tapped his fingers on the steering wheel. 'I'm going to rest my eyes for a bit.'

'He's not coming back, chéri.'

'You don't know that,' he said.

Chantelle tapped her temple. 'I have that feeling.'

Jack raised his eyebrows. 'All right, we'll give him another half hour.'

She nodded, for a moment lost in thought. Her fingers on the door handle, she opened it.

'Where are you going?'

'To look for a key.'

'I'm not sure about this, babe,' he said, turning off the engine and climbing out. He joined her as she headed to the front entrance.

Jack shook his head. 'It won't be under there.'

Chantelle crouched by the coir mat on the doorstep. 'That stink from the back. It is here too.' She gingerly pinched a corner between her thumb and forefinger. She let it fall. 'If he knew we were coming, that is where he would have left it.'

He shrank under her glare. 'Yes, I know. Or he wouldn't have gone out. I'm sorry, baby. I should have told him.'

'Your father, he has no burglar alarm?' Her gaze swept the line of outbuildings running the length of the house and beyond. 'He has padlocked all those doors except this one.'

Together, they approached and opened the door, recoiling at the sudden draught.

'That smell again,' Jack said. Through the gloom, he squinted at the gaping hole in the splintered timbers at the base of the far corner. 'Looks like he accidentally locked whatever that creature was in here.'

Chantelle flipped on the light and squeezed past him. 'It broke this wood in from the outside.' Her brow furrowed. 'But why? This is the woodshed, non?'

209

Jack shrugged. 'That's how it looks to me.'

She knelt to examine a tuft of matted black fur, plucking it from a jagged piece of wood. 'Look at this,' she said, handing it to him as she stood.

He held the clump under the lightbulb, feeling its texture. 'These hairs are long. Must be six inches.' He sniffed them. 'Cor, Jesus. Whatever is matting this together smells rotten.'

'Let me see.' Chantelle leaned closer. She took the fur, rolling it between her thumb and forefinger until a sticky dark residue appeared on her skin. 'I think it is blood.'

Jack flinched. 'I can't think of an animal native to here with a coat like that.'

'Perhaps it escaped from the zoo?'

'The nearest is in Edinburgh, but what could it be? A gorilla, a black bear.'

'The gorilla has no claws.' Her eyebrows knitted together. 'A bear is possible, but I do not think he has the hair like this.'

'Why are we speculating?' he said. 'When Dad turns up, we'll just ask him. Meanwhile, let's find a key to get in.'

Five minutes later, she rattled a bunch of keys in Jack's face.

'Where did you find them?'

'In this old biscuit tin and not only those, but look.'

'Wow,' he said, sifting through the collection of medals and certificates, scrutinising each one. 'I'd no idea he'd fought in so many places. Or that he was a captain….'

'Show me those photos,' she said.

210

'Why's he dumped them all out here to rot?' Jack scratched the back of his neck. 'They need to go inside.'

She crinkled her nose at the dank smell. 'I think your father, he wants to forget, non?'

Once inside the house, Jack quickly discovered his father's journal and began to read.

'There's some far-fetched nonsense in here,' he said.

'Like what?'

'He talks about the wolf and the strange highlander who visited him when I was seven….'

'The wolf in your nightmares began when your father told you of him, non?'

'Well, yes, I guess?' he said. 'Here he's talking about the crane and how the same stranger came and took her away… I mean, what's he doing?'

'It is a wonderful therapy to record our thoughts and dreams—'

'Not like this, babe. He actually believes it, I'm sure.' Jack shook his head, dismayed. 'Now he's talking about a beautiful woman who arrived dressed in nothing but fur, who couldn't remember a thing about herself? That's stretching it.'

'He means Anoushka?'

'I'm guessing so.'

'Let me see, chéri.'

Jack handed her the book.

Her eyes widened. 'You have not read it all?'

'Not yet, why?'

Chantelle looked at the floor. 'I cannot tell you. You must see for yourself.'

Jack tilted his head and searched her face. 'Baby, that doesn't sound good…'

She returned the book.

Jack chewed his lips as he pored over the page. 'Oh, Jesus Christ, he's definitely lost it.'

'I'm sorry, chéri, but your father is not here, and this book tells us where he might be—'

Jack wiped a tear from his eye. 'It does?'

'He speaks of a map where he thinks he will find the wolf.'

'I missed that. Couldn't take it all in.'

'The stranger gave it to him, non?'

'Babe, there is no map. How can there be?'

'Wait, what is that?' A ragged, yellowed edge protruded, thicker than the other pages.

'What on earth?' Jack tugged it out and unfolded the parchment-like paper. There in front of him, hand-drawn and clearly ancient, was the map.

The two of them gawped at each other in disbelief. Together, they studied the rest of the journal.

'He left two days ago.'

Chantelle read the intent on his face. 'Please, Jack, we call the mountain rescue.'

'No, baby. He planned to arrive today, the spring equinox. The journal said it would occur at 4:15 this afternoon.' Jack set the destination coordinates into his smartphone. 'That's where he'll be. I know it. We have about four hours to get there. We're going to drive as close as we can to where he's headed, and then I'll go on foot to find him. Start the car while I grab some better clothes.'

From the store cupboard in the hall, he grabbed as much mountain equipment as possible and rushed to join Chantelle in the car.

'Who are you calling?'

'No one,' he said. 'I'm switching on Google Maps.'

'You aren't relying on that?' She looked dismayed. 'What if you can't get a consistent phone signal?'

'I downloaded the maps back home, so we'd find the house without problems; otherwise, it would drain the battery constantly searching for a connection. GPS doesn't need a phone signal.' Jack shrugged. 'I'm not saying it will work, but if it doesn't, I grabbed one of Dad's ordnance maps.'

'We need to call Mountain Rescue, chéri.'

'Yes, call them.' He snapped the screenshot. 'I'm sending a photo of the coordinates. Give them these. You go back down while I see if I can find him.'

Chantelle watched him go. Phone in hand, he left the road, almost tripping over before he'd even started. She caught her breath. 'Mon Dieu, you are as stubborn as your father!'

213

As if he sensed her concern, Jack turned and waved.

She waved back.

In the distance, clouds obscured the mountains. Unable to connect to the emergency services during the journey from Jericho's house, she again tried. Nothing. Her mobile held at arm's length; she ran it in a circle while studying the screen for a signal. 'I shouldn't have let you go, chéri, not without knowing help is on the way.'

Jack had set his position to where they'd parked. She dared not move higher. She zipped her coat and got out. Walking close to the road's edge, she observed him as his form diminished against the valley. Why didn't they download a tracker so she could tell by his dot moving he was okay?

The air grew colder as she climbed higher, and the wind blew harder. After five hundred yards without success, she faced a dilemma.

A flurry of snow rushed across the road, pursued by an errant breeze. What if I don't get a signal no matter how high I climb?

Chantelle returned to the car.

Chapter 41

Jericho's trek, day two.

In the distance, the mountain crouched behind a veil of snow and cloud. Jericho squinted through the blizzard at his compass. The needle rotated 360 degrees, settled, and then lazily swung full circle again. Seized by a deep sense of déjà vu, his mind resurrected a long-forgotten memory.

Leading a troop of sixteen soldiers uphill through dense jungle, Jericho checked his bearings. His compass went haywire. Blake approached him and looked over his shoulder. 'Yours too, eh, sir?' he said. 'The men joke that it's something to do with that child exorcism we saw en route.'

'Unless the ceremony released a vast amount of magnetic energy, I think we can safely assume it's a natural phenomenon.'

'Have you experienced this situation before, sir?'

In Jericho's mind's eye, in another time and place, he squinted at his compass through the snow. *Why am I thinking I have when I know damn well I haven't?* Where two paths crossed, he again checked his instrument. Abruptly, the needle stopped moving. He inhaled deeply and closed his eyes. Instinct took over. 'This way, lads,' he said.

The line of men moved stealthily in the direction Jericho's compass point had stopped. He shivered. What lay ahead and how it would unfold, he hadn't yet figured out, but he sensed that, just like in Africa, it wasn't good.

He knew of areas like this all over the world, rocks which create magnetic fields leading the unwary traveller to certain doom in terrain and conditions like these. Jericho again gave himself over to instinct. In Africa, he had turned right. Suddenly, on this mountainside, he knew the way.

Through the vaporous swirl, he made out the unmistakable stovepipe rock formation. It was precisely as Fillan had described. *No way round or through, laddie, not like it was in my day.* No choice but to climb. At the foot of the crag, he looked up. The top shrouded from view; he knew to scale it now was suicidal. What choice do I have, old son? He took a deep breath, reached for a handhold and stepped up. A handhold secured, he shifted his weight and pulled up, beginning his precarious assault on the rock face.

Thirty minutes later, he could see neither the bottom nor the top through the swirling storm. He slowed to little more than a standstill, his hands, arms and legs knotted by the cold. No longer sure he possessed the endurance to make it to the top, disorientation set in. *If anyone can, my Jerry can.* Anita's voice seemed so loud and clear he turned to look for her. Catapulted through time to where they'd first met when he rescued Charlie from high on a castle ruin. The belief Anita was at his side spurred him on, and he climbed with renewed vigour.

The top crested, Jericho crawled clear of the edge, rolled onto his back, and stared up as myriad flakes floated like featherdown onto his face. Scooping a handful of snow, he crammed it greedily into his mouth. What he'd give to sleep right now. Closing his eyes, he teetered on the verge of consciousness. Another blast of wind would surely separate his spirit from his body. Like a home movie spliced together with no regard for time or sequence, the past flashed through his consciousness. The nightmare where Anita died. The children. Birdy. Anoushka. His lost youth. Memories like distant moons circumnavigated the black hole into which most of his life had fallen. The booze. Why had he not seen? He was the author of his own misfortunes, but wait. All that came after. After what? The answer lay in the darkness he refused to face. His heart fluttered as if starved of oxygen, then steadily sped up into an adrenaline-induced crazy rhythm.

Holy shit.

Faces streaked with camouflage paint, his troop split into four-man patrols. The soldiers looked primaeval, at odds with the combat fatigues, helmets and night vision goggles they wore. Under cover of darkness, they infiltrated a complex of adobe buildings surrounding a central stronghold.

They scooted from the shadows without firing a shot, slicing the throats of heavily armed guards. Young or old, it made no difference. Jericho's hands were slick with blood. The coppery smell of death was always the same.

Low chanting leaked from a house surrounded by charms and amulets. Inside, the target, a man who controlled his countrymen using juju, invoking suicide attacks just as hate preachers everywhere, except that for his believers, black magic was a more potent threat. *The witch doctor must die.*

Four men lined up, two on either side of the entry point, backs against the wall, awaiting Jericho's signal.

217

The chanting from within took on a menacing tone, reaching a fever pitch.

Jericho stepped up to the door and tried it. Locked. He drove his boot into it. Wood splintered, but it held firm. Shit!

Blake threw his shoulder against it, and it flew open. Christ, there's another door behind it. No point trying the handle. Somewhere in the house, unintelligible words screamed rapid-fire. Blake exchanged a glance with Jericho. In a well-rehearsed drill, together, they booted down the door. They stormed in, guns ready.

Backlit by flickering candles, sheets of cloth hung on lines stretched between the walls, dividing the room. The chanting stopped. The sheets billowed as if fanned by the breath of a sleeping giant.

'*Abandonner ou mourir,*' someone shouted. 'Surrender or die.'

The soldiers swept left and right, pie-slicing fields of vision, narrowing them, before entering the filthy curtained maze.

Jericho's heart pounded in his ears like a troop of Japanese drummers. He took a deep breath, gripped the edge of the cloth, and pulled it back.

Steel flashed. Blood spattered Jericho's face as his weapon came up.

A breeze rushed through the adobe structure; row after row of sheets fluttered with ominous violence. Something hit the floor and rolled towards Jericho. Simultaneously, a small body crumpled to the ground, blood gushing from its severed neck. A child. He let off a burst of automatic fire, aiming at the tall, dark figure standing in the shadows.

218

Fragments of ostrich feathers filled the air as round after round peppered the witch doctor, jerking him from side to side.

Why doesn't he fall? 'Die, you fucker,' Jericho screamed, tearing his target to pieces with deadly accuracy.

A single shot popped from next to him, punching a hole between its eyes. Blake stepped forward and plunged a knife into the broad chest, yanking it up and tearing through the feathered coat.

Stitched onto the juju man, a wolfs-head mask grinned in defiance.

'It's a fucking scarecrow!' Blake yelled.

Jericho stared at the broken child. 'The witch doctor... he did this.'

'But where did he go?' Blake searched his comrade's faces.

'He couldn't have got out, not past all of us,' Jones said.

Blake bared his teeth. 'Well, he ain't here now.'

'Get out there and find him!' Jericho sank to his knees and picked up the girl's head. An albino. He rose, cradling her in his arms like he was rocking her to sleep.

'Sir?' Blake approached him.

'This is on me,' Jericho murmured and wept.

'No.' Blake laid a gentle hand on his shoulder. 'He must've known we were coming, rigged a booby trap. The poor mite was dead the second he lifted the trapdoor to escape. There wasn't a thing you could do.'

'Where is he?'

'Spirited himself away,' Blake said. 'The lads are still looking for him.'

Stunned, Jericho opened his bleary eyes. Snow melting on his face mingled with salty tears. The journey home was a vague recollection without relevance now. A semblance of his life had resumed when Anita answered the door to him upon his return.

The wind died. The snowflakes grew larger. *Watch for the skelf...* A sharp inhale cleared his head. On the exhale, he rolled over and got to his feet, brushing his clothes down. I lost my way and found myself again. 'One more thing to do, old son,' he said through gritted teeth. 'Jericho Mathers does not go home until this job is done.'

Chapter 42

The hike was brutal, much harder than Jack expected. Three miles blitzed by icy winds and blinded by granulated snow, culminating in a thigh-sapping scramble up a steep rocky hillside.

On reaching the ridge, he knelt to catch his breath. After a minute, he rose to his feet and squinted ahead. In the fading daylight, the ravine he sought appeared, dark and foreboding as it snaked across the landscape.

'Thank God,' he whispered.

The caves couldn't be far away. For a moment, he pictured his father sheltering inside them, huddled over a fire, waiting out the storm. 'Man alive, Dad,' he said under his breath. 'This place is *cold.*'

He picked his way closer to the gorge, careful not to trip, straining ahead, looking for the landmark outcrop that concealed an entrance into a cave system.

A gust of wind slammed him from behind. Propelled towards the drop as if shoved by a giant hand, he threw himself down, hands and feet scrambling for purchase. This is it, he thought. Inches from the edge, his heel jarred against a rock. Another inch, and he'd have fallen into the abyss.

Heart hammering in his chest, Jack stared at the leaden sky and, taking a moment to gather his wits, rolled onto his knees and crawled away from the ledge. Once he was safe, he pulled out his GPS. His eyes blurred; he rubbed them and peered at the screen. A blinking green location marker almost overlapped the purple destination dot. Nearly there.

The wind whipped through his flapping jacket, chilling him to the bone. He braced himself and stood. Where's the crag? Oh, Christ. It's on the other side. His spirits sank as he weighed his choices. Backtracking was not an option.

Startled by a sudden movement, he stifled a gasp as a magnificent red stag trotted into view. Unaware of his presence, it smelled the air, raking the ground with a forehoof. Impulsively, he lifted his iPhone to take a picture. The beast raised his head. Through fogged breath, he and the stag stared at each other. Then, with a snort, it wheeled around and bolted. A split second later, a gunshot cracked.

Twenty yards away, a mound of snow-covered heather rose and shook like a dog coming out of a river. A green line scythed through the blizzard towards Jack. He lowered his gaze to his chest. A luminescent dot flickered over his heart.

A figure materialised out of the storm, as pixelated as a detuned image on an old analogue TV. Too big for a woman. Dressed in military-style camouflage, he wore a white ski mask with red stitching around the openings for his mouth and eyes. His rifle emitted a green laser beam.

The stranger stalked toward him, one of those tough-as-nails all-weather types. And a poacher, too. It was March, and the hunting season only lasted from July until October. Jack had a feeling he'd best not mention it.

'Hey there!' Jack yelled over the wind. 'Sorry about that. I didn't realise anyone else was up here.'

The man closed in, soldier-like, weapon up.

222

A spurt of adrenaline surged through Jack's veins. 'Can you put the gun down, please? You're making me nervous.'

The poacher continued his slow advance.

Jack blinked snow from his eyelids, breathed deep and lifted both hands. 'Look, I already apologised—'

'What the hell are you doing up here?' Anger infused the beady eyes.

'I'm looking for my father.'

High and shrill, the man mocked him. *Looking for my father.'*

Fear thickened Jack's tongue, the taste metallic. He thought frantically, seeking to defuse the man's anger. 'You're American?'

'Shut your fucking trap!' The black muzzle jabbed forward, stopping inches from Jack's face.

'Told me I'm making a big kill today, and that's what I aim to do.' His finger tightened on the trigger.

'Hey.' Jack took a backward step. 'Hey, don't do that. I have a wife and child,' he said, unashamed of the lie.

The man's lips appeared detached as they smirked. 'I told you to run.'

'Oh, come on—'

'Get. Running.'

'You won't get away with this.'

'So, I tell the cops that this guy pops up from nowhere between me and my stag just as I squeeze the trigger. You've got five seconds. Four, three...'

Jack's feet turned in the snow. He won't shoot this close, not if he can help it. If his accident story is to stack up, the poacher needs distance between us.

'Fucking move!' The man jabbed the rifle to make his point.

Without thinking, Jack grabbed the barrel and jerked it upward, stepping in simultaneously to smash an elbow into the man's jaw. The gun went off. The two grappled eyeball to eyeball, a series of grunts marking their exertion. His opponent pulled a knife. Jack seized him by the wrist and drove the top of his head into the masked face. The hunter fell backwards, Jack still controlling the gun and knife. He daren't let go. Another elbow strike followed by a well-placed knee. Jack wrenched the weapon away and, adjusting his grip, smashed the butt into the gritted teeth of his enemy. The man fell unconscious.

Jack searched the prone form and took possession of his knife and gun. For a few seconds, he considered the implications of leaving the American vulnerable to the elements. Should I tie him? The guy has no qualms about threatening me, he thought. Besides, he had to find his father. He raised the gun and peered through the telescopic sight, adjusting the scope for clarity as he scanned the clifftop on the opposite side.

Across the ravine, below his line of sight, Jericho appeared.

'Hey, Dad,' he yelled, waving his arms. 'It's me, Jack. Wait. I'm coming over,'

Something dark and monstrous closed in on his father. He quickly sighted the rifle and sharpened the lens' focus. 'No way,' he gasped. Suddenly breathless and with trembling hands, he took a moment to steady his aim. He fired.

Chapter 43

A shot echoed around the mountainside. Jericho rushed to the mouth of the cave. An instinct, long dormant, awoke in him. In a kind of trigonometric diagnosis, he rapidly determined the shot came from the other side of the ravine. Ducking low, he crept to the edge of the precipice. What the fuck? Across the valley, a figure stood, rifle aimed at him. A bullet whooshed past before the clap of the second shot. Instinctively, he dropped flat on the ground. The shooter was now yelling. Another shot. Whoever it is, is warning me. Something familiar about the voice? Behind you, Dad! Sounds like Jack, but how can it be? Distracted, he did not notice the dark shape creeping up on him. At the last moment, Jericho turned. The wolf leapt for him.

Jack gasped. Terrified, he had no choice but to watch helplessly as the attack unfolded through the lens of the telescopic sight. There was no clear shot. He cannot risk it. Maybe the report crashing between the valley walls would frighten the animal, but in his heart, he knew it would not. The wolf stood on its hind legs, a foot taller than his father, the monstrous head savagely wrenching from side to side. Jericho had both hands clenched deep into the wolf's mane, struggling to hold it off. Back and forth, they wrestled, beast and man edging closer to the edge of the cliff.

'Kick it,' Jack yelled.

As if on cue, his father drove a knee hard into its belly.

The wolf pushed back. Caught off balance, Jericho lost his footing and slipped closer to the precipice.

'Jesus, Dad!'

In the next instant, Jack's head exploded in a starburst of colours. His legs buckled while he half-spun, feet dancing a crazy two-step. The hunter snatched the rifle from his hands. 'Now you're gonna pay.'

Jack winced in pain. 'Wait,' he said, gingerly touching his head, feeling warm blood trickle down his neck. 'You wanted to shoot something big? Shoot that wolf over there before it pushes my dad over the cliff.'

'That trick is as old as the hills,' the poacher said. 'On your knees—'

'You have three seconds to bag the biggest black wolf you ever saw. At least *look.*'

The man raised the gun, sighted down the barrel and whistled. 'What the hell?'

'Kill it,' Jack said. 'Just don't hit my dad.'

'Its got him by the throat. Looks like he's fucked as far as I can tell.'

'Just shoot it, for Christ's sake!'

Pinned under the wolf, Jericho dug his chin into the crook of his elbow. The creature clamped its jaws, fangs penetrating his jacket sleeve, digging into the flesh of his left forearm. Tasting blood, the wolf threw its head from side to side, growling savagely, tearing deeper, grating on bone. Fuelled by and anaesthetised by adrenaline, he

227

disregarded the pain. Unable to fend the creature off, he calculated his chances. If he let go of the mane and reached for the blade in his boot, could he fatally stab his nemesis before it rendered his protective arm useless? If I don't take the chance, I'm dead, and if I do and it kills me, at least I tried. Jericho threw his body to one side, hoping to roll the beast, but failed. Praying for a miracle, he released his grip and grabbed the knife.

The wolf tore into him with renewed vigour. Triumph in its wild eyes, it flipped Jericho onto his belly and attacked his exposed nape.

Jericho stabbed backwards blindly, unable to penetrate the vital parts of the animal atop him. Desperation took over, and he thrust upward, pushing against the massive weight bearing down on him. Slowly, he stood, the wolf's paws still wrapped around his neck while it began to gnaw at the back of his skull. He turned, kicked back on a rock, and elbowed the beast's abdomen hard. The two of them fell perilously close to the edge. He had to break free and stab the monster in the eye like Fillan told him. For a moment, Jericho stared into the sky. High above, little more than a speck, white and cruciform, something wheeled in a short arc and disappeared behind the clouds. His strength ebbed away. Memories flashed like movie reels sucked into a vortex, spinning out of control. No longer in pain, he sagged.

The wolf's eyes gleamed, victorious.

'Looks like your old man's given up,' the hunter said.

'Take the shot!' Jack yelled.

The gunman took aim. His finger tightened on the trigger.

228

Above, clouds parted. A golden shaft of sunshine beamed directly onto wolf and man.

Suddenly, from out of the sky, plunging at great speed, head forward, wings tucked back, a snow-white bird gilt by the sun, guided by the power of light, slammed into the wolf.

'Holy mother of God,' the hunter cried. 'Did you see that bird? It just speared the wolf right in the eye with its beak.'

Jericho rolled over. The wolf lay motionless. Blood flowed from where its eye had been.

'Birdy?' Jericho whispered.

The crane hesitated, stared at him for a long moment, and then, with a hop, skip, and mighty leap, took off again. Up and up she flew, Jericho's teary eyes trailing her.

With enormous effort, he heaved the wolf to the rim and sat back against the rocks, using both feet to push it into oblivion. He peered over the edge in time to see the beast bounce off the jagged cliff twice, cartwheeling down onto a sapling that bent, breaking its fall before snapping and impaling the wolf through the chest.

Jericho flopped onto his back and looked up. The bird circled the sky one last time and was gone. His eyes drooped, then shut. A voice came to him from afar. He couldn't make it out. Golden light, warm and welcoming, beckoned him. He drifted. I'm coming home, Neet.

A faint voice called him back. 'Dad, Dad! Are you all right?'

'Jack,' he whispered. 'Where's Emily?'

In the distance, a helicopter approached.

Chapter 44

Six weeks later. Melbourne, Australia.

Emily drank tea, looking out of the window over her front garden.

'Can you believe that this time next bloody week, you'll be a married woman?' Kurt said, towelling sweat from his forehead.

'It seems unreal.' She sipped her drink.

'You looking forward to it?'

'I wish I knew for sure Dad was coming.'

'What did the hospital say?'

'They said he can't travel.'

'We can always send him the video?'

'Kurt, we should have postponed.'

'If you feel that strongly, we still can.'

'He insisted we don't.'

'There you go,' he said. 'What time are we collecting the dress?'

'After lunch.'

'Come on, Ems, let's get outta here. Go into town early. Grab a bite, maybe a beer?'

'I'm fine, honestly, but whatever happens, you'd best shower first.'

'Bloody cheek,' he said.

A taxi pulled up over the road. Two soldiers got out.

Seeing them, Kurt said, 'Give the old man a call?'

She instinctively glanced at her watch. 'It's ten at night over there. I'm not hindering his recuperation.'

'If you won't, I bloody will. Pass us your phone.'

She gestured to the coffee table. 'It's there on the side.'

'He won't answer, anyway.'

'Not if he doesn't want to.'

'Did Jack ever tell you the full story?'

She laughed. 'Are you kidding? Talk about the apple doesn't fall far from the tree.'

'So, he goes out climbing in a blizzard, and your brother found him at the foot of a cliff?'

'That's the story,' she said.

'I'm glad those nightmares of yours stopped.'

'Not as much as me.' Emily looked thoughtful. 'I must ask Jack if his ones have too. Is it ringing?'

'It won't go through?'

The doorbell rang. Emily craned her neck around the curtains and dashed to the door.

'It's Dad,' she cried.

'I didn't think you were coming, the hospital…'

Jericho grinned. 'I discharged myself.'

Emily reached for his neck.

He shied away. 'What're you doing?'

'What really happened, Dad?'

'Didn't Jack tell you I fell?'

'The nurse I spoke to said the injuries were consistent with bites—'

'Talk to your brother when you see him next week. He saw it all.'

'I know you aren't telling me everything, but hey, you must be exhausted. Here, let Kurt take your suitcase.'

'You're here! That's why the bloody call wouldn't go through. How are you, Jerry?'

He winced a little at Kurt's familiarity. 'I can manage, mate,' he said and handed Emily a parcel from under his arm.

'What's this?' she said.

'Open it and see… but not in front of your fiancé.'

'Oh, that's nice,' Kurt said. 'I'll go make a cuppa. Want one, Jerry?'

Jericho watched as Emily unwrapped the gift and lifted the lid. Her eyes shone, 'Oh my God, Dad, it's beautiful.' She ran her hands over the material. 'It's so lush. I've never felt anything as soft in my life.'

'Try it on,' he said.

'I've already ordered a dress—'

'Cancel it.'

'Oh, Dad. I couldn't let them down....'

'Try it. If it fits, then choose. If you prefer the other, it's fine, really.'

Jericho waited outside her room while she changed.

The door opened. Emily's eyes brimmed with tears as she stepped out.

'You look absolutely gorgeous in it, Ems.'

'This is the best thing I've ever put on in my life. I'm not even joking; it's magical. The material is so fine. Where did you get it?'

Jericho touched his nose.

'But what's it made with?'

Jericho felt like Scrooge on Christmas morning, finally freed of the shackles which dogged him all his life. No more would he exclude himself from his family and friends. 'What's it made with?' Suddenly overcome, he choked back a sob, cleared his throat and said tenderly, 'Love, Ems. It was made with love.'

The End

About the author

Max China is the pen name of a British writer of mystery and suspense thrillers with a penchant for crime, often infused with a supernatural flavour. The author of four novels to date and numerous short stories. His debut novel The Sister charted at number one in many Amazon categories on its 2013 release.

His books sell internationally.

More from the author

Novels by Max China

Where Did You Go?

The Sister

The Life and Times of William Boule

The Night of the Mosquito

Don't Turn on the Light

The Sister Redux

Short stories

Whatever Happened to Becky Leigh?

Night Nurse

A Fresh Start

Short Story Extract

A Fresh Start

Luke Masterson gazed from the window of the bedroom he'd once shared with his older brother, remembering the night he failed to come home.

Seven years ago, today.

Police at the doorstep.

Mum collapsed, wailing. 'No. Not Luther. Not my Luther.'

Luke's hot tears and Dad's incandescent rage.

Seven years. Luke withdrew completely, and it was twelve months before he spoke again and another year of therapy before his psychiatrist coaxed him from the prison of his own making, leaving the demons locked inside.

Only one visible throwback remained of those dark days. Trichotillomania. Obsessive hair pulling. They warned him it could come and go, but it had never entirely gone. Raking his dirty-blonde mane with his fingers, he paused, isolated a single strand, and pulled it out by the root. Time was, he'd have continued to pluck until a penny-sized bald patch appeared on his scalp. Now, another tug, and he'd be at the edge, a step closer to falling back into the cycle of shame and remorse. Luke exhaled slowly, allowing the hair to fall to the floor.

'Lukie,' his mother said, entering the room. 'Let's not do this.'

Luke half-turned toward her. 'I'm not going to work today.'

'Come here.' Mum stepped forward, pulling him into her arms. 'I miss your brother too, but you mustn't let people down like that,' she said. 'You'll be better off there, keeping occupied. Believe me.'

'I just can't do it.' Luke pulled away.

'Yes, you can,' she insisted. 'You're twenty-three, Lukie. You've achieved a lot since... you know.'

'Is it wrong to want time for myself before I return to uni?'

'No, it isn't, but if you are serious about backpacking, you need the money.'

'If I'm serious?' Luke reached for his hair. Mum's gaze followed. Their eyes met. Her head shook imperceptibly. His hand stopped at his beard and scratched it as if that had been his intention all along.

'I'd be happier if you went with a friend. I'm not sure you're ready.'

'You always have to make me doubt myself,' he said.

'I don't doubt you for a minute, but...' she said, 'the world's a dangerous place.'

'I'll be fine.' Luke glanced at his watch. 'Oh shit. I won't make it to work on time now.'

238

'Don't worry,' Mum said. 'You can borrow my car. If you hurry, you'll arrive with time to spare.'

'I've been thinking a lot about Dad lately. I know what he did was wrong,' Luke paused by the front door, 'but we never talk about him...'

'He's refused to see us for six years.' Her eyes misted and drifted to the floor as if following the progress of a handful of falling feathers. 'I don't know how I feel anymore.'

'In a misguided way, he did what he did for us...'

Her gaze returns to him, defiant. 'It was selfish. Just when we needed him most.' She dabbed her wet eyelashes with a tissue. 'There's no time now. Let's get through the day, and we'll talk later, yes?'

He squeezed her hand and left.

Luke stopped the yellow Ford Fiesta in the car park of The Albion pub. Ready for his shift, he visualised his mother, alone at home crying as she often did, but today of all days? He shouldn't have listened. Should have stayed with her. 'Too wrapped up in your backpacking trip,' he said, and grabbing two fists full of hair, gritted his teeth, determined to inflict pain on himself. A sound like grass being torn from the ground stopped him. 'Why do I always have to feel this way?'

The only other vehicle there, five bays over from Luke's, was a battered white van with blacked-out windows parked askew across two spaces. The owner, he guessed, was probably still asleep in the back after a skinful the night before.

Luke glanced at his watch: 9:35 am. He looked in the rearview mirror and tilted his head, first one way, then the other, teasing his hair back into shape.

Frank appeared at the front door. A bull of a man, he yelled, 'Come on, you wanker. Stop pissin' about over there. You got work to do, and you're already fuckin' late.'

A surge of adrenaline set Luke's stomach swirling. Only a few more days of this, he reminded himself and got out of the car.

Frank beckoned him over. 'That's a nice new motor. Obviously payin' you too much. Or you're nickin' off me?'

'Like I'd steal enough in six weeks without you noticing,' Luke said. 'Seriously, it's my mum's.'

'So you say,' Frank said. 'Here. Catch.'

A fist-sized bunch of keys arced twenty feet through the air towards him, the sun momentarily glinting on the bright array of metals. The writhing mass caught Luke off guard as a massive F-shaped brass fob swung axe-like through his fingers, chopping down hard against the back of his hand. 'Shit,' he said under his breath. 'That fucking hurt, you fat —'

'What did you say?' Frank said through clenched teeth.

'Nothing,' Luke mumbled, looking down at his shoes. 'I asked you where you're going?'

Frank glared at him. 'A real man says what he says and stands by it. Remember that.' He headed down the access road to the loading area. 'I've got to fix them cellar doors. Won't be long. Lock the door behind you.'

Luke set about his duties. He dreaded Monday mornings. They invariably brought an assortment of characters in from

240

far and wide. Soon, the locals would start a queue to get in. Pissheads. All of them.

Twenty minutes later, Luke emptied the dishwasher and polished smears from the glasses while thinking about the travel itinerary Luther never had the chance to fulfil. At night, they'd talked about the far-flung places he planned to visit. Images of Marrakesh, the Himalayas, and Cambodia's temples vied for his attention. He pictured him sporting the Muay Thai tattoos he'd promised himself from Thailand, striding along a dusty trail under a dazzling sun, weighed down by a backpack, map in hand, nonchalant, untroubled by solitude because that was his big brother. It wouldn't be long before Luke set out on the journey, a kind of homage to Luther. Had he the backbone for it? Maybe not yet, but he knew his brother would be there with him in spirit every step of the way. And this was his chance to commune with him, to continue his healing.

Someone hammered on the front door, interrupting Luke's train of thought.

'Hurry, you wanker.' Frank yelled. 'I don't have all day.'

Luke's mood sank. He scooped the keys and walked over to unlock. 'Christ, Frank. You frightened the life outta me, banging on the door like that. You could've just walked up through the cellar.'

'It's locked from this side, and I didn't have these, genius.' He grabbed the keys. 'Bolt the door after me. I'm goin' back down to the cellar to check everything's locking properly from the inside now. Shouldn't take long.'

Luke cast an eye over the pub. Filled with old oak beams and nooks and crannies, the red ceiling and the nicotine-yellowed walls did nothing to brighten the place. If you closed your eyes, you could almost smell the fug of cigarette smoke from yesteryear. A few glasses here and there remained on tables uncollected from the previous night. Unlike Frank to retire to bed before he'd checked the place was tidy, he thought.

This would be the first time he'd opened the establishment without Frank or his wife present. Sometimes, Bella wouldn't come down at all. He'd once glimpsed her at the base of the stairs. She turned away quickly, but not before Luke saw the expression of shame on her battered and swollen face. After that, he sometimes fantasised about helping her escape, but lacked the courage. When he didn't see her again for the best part of two weeks, Luke finally enquired about her.

'Women's problems,' Frank said tersely.

On the dark oak beam over the opening into the lounge, the second hand of a railway clock entered the final minute before ten. Luke grabbed the remote and turned on the television. The screen came to life in the middle of a news bulletin.

'A string of pub robberies throughout Essex culminated in five brutal murders last night with what detectives described as a bloodbath in a local public house,' the presenter said. 'We're now going over live to the scene.'

The camera panned over a mountain of flowers, the bouquets stacked next to the car park wall, taking in forensic tents, the flashing lights of police and emergency vehicles behind, a busy crime scene delineated by blue and white tape criss-crossing the area behind before settling on a female journalist holding a microphone up to a sombre-faced detective.

'This is Detective Constable George Dunbar, who's in charge of the investigations,' she said. 'What can you tell us so far?'

'We're following up on several enquiries; however, we believe the same person to be responsible for this–and the previous pub robberies in the county.' The DC blinked, his voice slightly out of sync with his on-screen image. 'We think the suspect entered the Dick Turpin public house at or around closing time....'

Thank God I don't work nights, thought Luke. Through the front window, he spotted a group of regulars crossing the road to the Royal Oak opposite. It could be they had an early bird special. Sometimes, Frank ran such a promotion when things were quiet.

Luke unbolted the main door, securing it open against the wall with a cabin hook.

A single customer stepped over the threshold. A tall, gaunt-faced man dressed in dirty jeans and a charcoal pinstriped suit jacket. Pushing lank black hair away from his forehead, he dropped to one knee to tighten a bootlace while Luke walked on. 'Whiskey,' he called out. 'Irish. Make it a double.'

'Got it,' Luke said as he ducked through the counter flap.

The stranger lowered his head beneath the bar's over-counter and walked the length of it, inspecting the bottles lined up against the mirrored rear wall. 'No Jameson?'

'It's round the corner in the snug bar. I'll go get it.'

The stranger followed him.

'Bit early for a double, isn't it?' Luke said, raising an eyebrow.

243

The stranger's voice lowered. 'Ye judging me?'

'No,' Luke said. 'Just being sociable.'

The stranger squinted at Luke's name tag. 'No, ye weren't, Luke.' His forefinger flicked the tip of his broken nose with unnecessary force. 'Fuckin' nosy. That's what ye are. Now get me that drink, or do I have to pour it meself?'

Luke saw the front door was now closed. 'Mister,' he said, pointing to the entrance. 'I left that open. Why did you shut it?'

'I don't like the light, see?' The stranger said. 'Does me head in. So, ye getting me that whiskey, or what?'

Luke pumped the spirit dispenser and, catching movement in the mirrored wall behind the bottle display, frowned.

Old John Davey peered through the front window, hands framing his face against the glass. From Luke's vantage point, he figured John couldn't see into the snug where he and the stranger stood unless he looked into the exact same spot in the mirror as Luke. After a few moments, John turned away and crossed the car park toward the pub over the road.

His focus shifted to the stranger's reflection. They made eye contact. Luke broke off and spun around to place the drink on the bar. 'There you go,' he said. 'Nine pounds and eighty pence, please.'

''Bout fuckin' time.' The stranger snatched up the whiskey and drained it at a tilt. 'Another,' he said and slammed the glass onto the bar.

Luke's tongue flicked over suddenly parched lips. 'You gotta pay for that first.'

'Do I indeed?' The stranger thrust out his stubbled chin and glared. One eye was bloodshot, and the other gleamed as sharp as a gimlet. 'Put it on the tab.'

'The landlord doesn't allow that,' Luke said.

'It's only us, boy, and I say what goes.'

'Frank won't have it.' Luke started for the bar flap. 'I'm going to have to check with him.'

'No need.' The stranger moved to block Luke in with deceptive nimbleness. 'He knows me.'

'I still have to run it past him.' Luke lifted the access flap.

'Did ye not hear me just now?' The stranger grabbed the edge, easily overcoming Luke's upward motion to force it back down. 'He's not the man ye think he is….'

'Who, Frank?'

'Yep.'

'What do you mean?' Luke said.

'Aaaah, nothin'.'

'What's the name?'

'Are ye a fuckin' copper now, is it?'

'Look,' Luke said. 'Frank'll kill me if you don't pay as you go.'

'I told ye. It's fine.'

A burst of adrenaline threatened to loosen Luke's bowels. 'I still want your name.'

'I don't suppose it makes much difference…' He leaned

across the bar so close that Luke smelled the stale-biscuit griminess of his hair and clothes.

'It's Spider.' He tapped the scorpion tattoo on the back of his hand. 'Now pour that whiskey. The day's not gettin' any younger, and me patience is wearin' thin.'

'I'm a Scorpio,' Luke said. 'I reckon you probably are as well. Otherwise, why the tattoo?'

'And ye think that makes us kin or somethin'?'

'No, but it's something in common.' Luke lifted the tumbler from Spider's hand.

'Well, ye're wrong. We ain't alike at all. Stupid plummy-voiced fuckin' rich kid.'

'Me?' Luke dispensed two shots from the optic and handed the glass back. 'You know nothing about me.'

Spider raised his eyebrows, a hint of amusement on his lips. 'Is that so?'

'Yeah,' Luke said.

'Ye're a fuckin' coward.'

'I can't see how you can say that—'

'How? I'll tell ye how. I heard the man calling ye a wanker, and what did ye say?'

Luke hung his head. 'I didn't say anything.'

A silence descended between them. Each alone in their thoughts.